Lily

CHRIS KENISTON

Indie House Publishing

Indie House Publishing

BOOKS BY CHRIS KENISTON

Surf's Up Flirts
(Aloha Series Companions)
Shall We Dance
Love on Tap
Head Over Heels
Perfect Match
Just One Kiss
It Had to Be You

**Other Books
By Chris Keniston**

Honeymoon Series
Honeymoon for One
Honeymoon for Three

Family Secrets Novels
Champagne Sisterhood
The Homecoming
Hope's Corner

Original Aloha Series
Waikiki Wedding

ACKNOWLEDGEMENTS

Has everyone figured out that I could not write a series of books without the help of a whole lot of good friends? Well, it's true. For a lot of reasons this series has been an extra challenge for me to write and I am eternally grateful to so many people.

First I want to thank Cindy Dees for the wonderful 'meet cute' idea. Worked like a charm. Next I want to thank my Aunt Mary for bringing my cousin's favorite cookies all the way to Texas – long live spitzbubens! I owe a special thank you to Barb Han for showing up faithfully at my house three days a week and making sure the pages got written – you rock!

Last but not certainly not least, I want to thank my review team for all the love. In every book I've told readers how important reviews are to authors. With this series in particular I've had to work twice as hard to get words on the page, and so many of the words were inspired after a kind pre-release review from my team members! You guys are the very best!

Happy reading!

"It will never work."
"Of course, it will."
"As much as I'd like to think you're right, I don't know."
"Well, I do. Sit back and see for yourself."

CHAPTER ONE

Flames thrashed at the charred walls. Time was running out. Pushing through the thick black smoke, Cole McIntyre made his way down the second floor hall of the small high school, checking and clearing each and every classroom along the way. According to the teachers huddled outside, there was one teacher and possibly two or three students trapped behind the fire line. Even in the few minutes it had taken them to weave through the afternoon traffic, the small fire had grown to engulf half the building.

Every thirty seconds this monster was doubling in size. Despite the protective gear, Cole could feel the heat beating at his back. What a mess. The snap of crumbling wood sounded overhead. A flaming beam came crashing down, sending him jagging left—fast.

"Cole!" His partner's voice sounded in his ear.

Flashing a thumbs up, Cole pressed forward. Neither able to see more than a few feet in front of them, he'd counted doors and had to be approaching the chemistry lab at the end of the hall. A student who had escaped from the lab reported the flash fire had climbed instantly to the ceiling and rapidly traveled toward the back wall, trapping the teacher and whoever had been sitting nearby. Afraid to cross through the flames, the teacher herded the children to temporary safety in a storage room. He hoped to God the door was made of steel.

In an attempt to contain the fire, several teachers had pulled the doors closed behind them on their way out of the building. The chem lab had been no exception. Kicking the door down and staying low, he followed the wall around for reference. The outside team had been watering down this area but the lab was still a hot spot. Heart rate pounding, he came to the storage room and shoved the door open.

In the opposite corner, the teacher and one student lay close to the ground. Before he could reach them, the two crawled, one hand holding their faces, in his direction. They were alive. Now came the fun part—getting them the hell out of the building.

• • • •

"I. Am. Not. Frustrated." Lily Nelson blew a wisp of hair away from her face and slammed her fist into the gooey mound in front of her.

"Call it what you want." Hands on her hips, Lucy, the family's longtime housekeeper, cook, and avid *Hello Dolly* fan, stared at her with cool indifference. "I've watched you bake bread before and you don't usually pound at the dough with quite so much murderous intent."

Lily flipped and folded the dough, making a conscious effort to not hammer at it as if it were Danny Fluegel's face.

"I don't suppose you want to tell me why you're baking bread here at this hour?"

"This kitchen is bigger than Mom's." The timer sounded and wiping her hands on her apron, Lily crossed the room, ignoring the woman standing guard like a drill sergeant at boot camp, and peeked into the oven. Perfection. Using her apron for mitts, she maneuvered the hot tray onto the cooling rack and spun back to the raw dough.

So what if she baked when she had too much on her mind? So what if Danny Fluegel went out last night with featherbrained—and stacked—Kathleen Barker? It's not like they were in a committed relationship. Heck, after only three dates in three weeks she wasn't even sure it counted as a relationship. And, even if he was perfect-picture- handsome, after two rather wilted kisses, she hadn't even been sure she wanted a fourth date.

What she wanted was her own bakery. A place to create all the delectable flavors swirling in her head for the rest of the world to taste and enjoy. Or at least all of Lawford Mountain not staying at the Hilltop Inn. And Margaret O'Malley's Boutique on Main Street would be the perfect spot. Just not this year. She punched the dough again.

"Oh, my." Either not noticing or choosing to overlook the last act of violence on the innocent pile of raw dough, Lucy inched closer to the warm French breakfast fare, sniffed the air as though she were a blood hound on the hunt, and moaned softly. "I have no idea what has sent you into baker-on-steroids mode, but I do love your croissants. Is that extra butter I smell?"

Lily might have gotten a little heavy handed with the butter. But to her, butter was the basis of all great comfort foods. And tonight she felt like comfort.

Visiting from Boston, her cousin Violet stopped short in the doorway. "Do I smell croissants?"

"With extra butter." Lucy snuck a pinch of the steaming warm flaky temptation.

Lily blew out a sigh and returned her fingers to the dough.

"You going to bake that or beat five pounds out of it?" Violet pinched a morsel of croissant for herself. A yoga instructor, her cousin had the calm Zen life down pat. "Cause if you need to get rid of some of that frustration, I could show you—"

"I am *not* frustrated." Miffed. Disappointed, maybe. But not frustrated. Not really. Maybe. All right. Who was she kidding? Self-absorbed men like Danny were made for the Barbie look-alikes in this world. She should have known better than to let Lucy set her up, but with Heather and Jake looking so insanely happy, and her not having been on a single date in two years, she might have been a bit too willing to overlook Lucy's track record. Being dumped—sort of—by him wouldn't have bothered her at all if she didn't see her biggest chance at her own bakery slipping away.

"Then tell me why you look like your soufflé fell?" Barefoot, dressed in comfy yoga pants and an oversized t-shirt, her cousin leaned against the counter, silently waiting for Lily to explain her late night baking marathon.

Heaving a sigh, she dropped the dough in a bowl, covered it with a towel, and turned to her audience of two. "Danny Fluegel is seeing Kathleen Barker."

"The man has no taste." Lucy stuffed another piece of croissant in her mouth as if she hadn't been the one to set Lily and Danny up in the first place.

Violet frowned. "I thought he was a bad kisser?'

"He is."

"Then I don't understand." The frown remained intact.

"It's just…" What? Danny. No. That was a handy excuse. If only the timing wasn't all wrong.

Shaking her head and smiling, Lucy came up to Lily and patted her hand before stepping away again. "If it makes you feel any better, we've got a few bookings coming up with new guests. Including a handsome fireman."

"Lucy," Lily practically groaned

"What?" Lucy's not so innocent eyes opened wide. "You have anything against good looking firemen?"

"Of course not. But I don't want you saying—or doing—anything that I'm going to regret." *Again*. Lucy may think herself the matchmaker extraordinaire but there was no denying how terrible she was at it. Not only, like Danny, did her choices not pan out, her methods were questionable. Last summer the woman had actually tripped Amy Crowder at the Fourth of July barbecue so Lucy could insist the new—six foot two, blue eyed, good looking—EMT take a look at Amy's not sprained ankle. She didn't need Lucy arranging yet another date for her with a self-absorbed, too-handsome for his own good, member of the male species. Someone could get hurt.

"Me?" Lucy had the audacity to flatten her palm against her chest and look surprised at being called out on her matchmaking shenanigans. "I haven't done a thing. A fire department representative will stay with us for a week to decide if Hart Land would be a good spot for the annual firefighter's retreat. Between the lake views, my cooking, and your baking, there isn't a snowball's chance under the sun that the retreat won't be held here."

On the surface that seemed like a legitimate reason for having a firefighter in one of the rental cabins. After all, ever since his class reunion several months ago, her grandfather, retired Marine Corps General Harold Hart, had been practically living on the computer, strategizing new marketing efforts, the same way she suspected he would have planned the invasion of an enemy country. Both of which, she had no doubt, he would be successful at. On the other hand, this was Lucy.

Pulling apart another croissant, the housekeeper paused mid-tear and grinned. "Can you imagine all those good looking firemen scattered across Hart Land for days?"

"*Luuucy*," Lily enunciated carefully.

The older woman swiped another croissant and turned away, mumbling, "Sometimes I think you girls are the baby boomers and your Grams and I are the younger generation."

"Well, you're both certainly young at heart, I'll give you that." And that was all Lily was going to say. Otherwise Lucy was capable of setting a cabin on fire so the big strong firemen could rescue her damsel in distressed self.

Waiting a beat for Lucy to be out of earshot, Violet cleared her throat. "Okay, it's just the two of us. What's really eating at you and don't tell me it's Danny because I'm not buying."

"Okay." Lily sank onto a stool and considered if half past eleven was too late to test a new recipe for butterscotch cookies she'd been thinking about. *Oh just spit it out.* "Margaret O'Malley is retiring."

"Heaven knows she's probably older than dirt." Having grown up in Boston, Violet and her two sisters had spent every summer at the lake and knew all the locals as well as any resident of Lawford.

"She told Mom that without Herbie, running the shop just wouldn't be the same. She's going to close the boutique." Lily reached for a croissant.

"That's wonderful." Violet leaped forward and stopped short at Lily's expression. "Isn't it? I mean, you've been dreaming of your own bakery on Main Street for years."

Dreaming was the key word. Since returning from studying in France she'd scrimped and saved, moved in with her mom, and to save even more money, spent most of her free evenings on her grandparent's porch playing cards with the retired generation and miscellaneous cabin guests. Getting out the last few weeks—even with Danny Fluegel—had been a nice change.

"I give," Violet said. "Why isn't this good news? The shops on Main Street never turn over. We all thought it would be years before you got your chance."

Years. It seemed that might be how long it could take to find that one signature item to set her apart from the rest of the bakeries in the state. Seeking the elusive standout cupcake, cookie, cake, or bread recipe, this kitchen had been through more experiments than a high-tech chemistry lab searching for a cancer cure. With the cost of remodeling and no single standout marketable hook, she didn't have enough savings to keep her afloat past the first year. If that. "It's just not the best timing."

"Timing?"

"I'm not ready."

"Ready?" Violet's eyes circled round with surprise. "You do remember you're a graduate of the best cooking school in Paris? You've been ready for this since you were eight years and old and got your first Easy Bake Oven."

That made her smile. "Ten and my second Easy Bake Oven. I wore out the first one."

"See. You can do this. If you want to."

Yeah. She wanted to. Boy, did she want to.

● ● ● ●

"Man, that could have been so much worse." Cole's partner Payton guzzled a bottle of cool water.

Cole dropped hard onto the wooden chair in the kitchen. "What's the point of the US Chemical Safety Board—a federal agency—warning against using methanol in laboratory and school demonstrations if the teachers aren't going to pay any attention?"

Rolling the cool bottle across his forehead, Payton shrugged. "Don't ask me, ask the school board."

"At least she had the good sense to block the bottom of the door with towels."

"Didn't hurt any that they were breathing through…what was

it?"

"A cotton slip." Cole had to give the woman credit for staying calm in a situation that would have sent most people into a deadly panic. "She'd taken hers off and torn it in pieces for them to breathe through."

Payton narrowed his eyes. "I thought only grandmothers wore those things."

"Apparently not."

"Whatever." Payton jumped to his feet and crossed to the stove. "My stomach is about to kiss my backbone. How much longer?"

Derrick, the firefighter in charge of dinner tonight, didn't bother answering. He just shot Payton an annoyed glare, much like a big brother would to his nuisance younger sibling.

Swiping a slice of bread from the basket on the counter, Payton turned back to his partner. "So how did you get this sweet assignment?"

"What assignment?" Gabe, the charmer of the firehouse, came to a stop by the kitchen table.

Payton waived his thumb at Cole. "This one is spending an all expenses paid week's stay on the Hart property by the lake."

Gabe whistled. "I'm with Bruiser here. How'd you finagle that?"

"I didn't finagle anything. Captain asked if I'd volunteer a day off to inspect all the smoke alarms on the property. Next thing I know, the old guy—"

"You mean the General?" Derrick asked.

Cole nodded. "That would be the one. Followed me around closer than my shadow. Any minute I thought the guy was going to tell me how to do my job."

"You mean he didn't?" Derrick looked surprised.

"Nope. He frowned, harrumphed a few times, might have cracked a hint of a smile a time or two, but refrained from critiquing my performance." Before any of the guys could come back with a wise crack, he responded, "And no comments from the peanut gallery. My *performance* is just fine."

"All I know," Derrick pulled out the chair beside him, "is that when I did that inspection two years ago the guy was worse than white on rice. Questioned if I needed a different screwdriver—a *screwdriver*—then he questioned the accuracy of the meters. Anyone would have thought testing smoke alarms required a PhD in rocket science."

Cole chuckled. "Maybe you have a dishonest face?"

Turning away from Derrick, Payton swallowed a grin. Cole would have expected him to be the first to jump on a line like that.

"Hardy har har," Derrick flashed a toothy smile. "I haven't heard of anyone ever getting invited back, never mind invited to stay for a week."

"It's not like he wants to play poker with me. Hart House wants the retreat business."

"And what," Gabe frowned, "would you have to do with that?"

Cole shrugged. "Honestly, I don't know. I was just as shocked as you guys are when the captain called me into his office to inform me of the stay."

"Isn't it against department policy to accept gifts?" Derrick ran a hand across the back of his neck. "I mean, a week's stay at a popular lakeside vacation spot, even between peak seasons, is one hell of a gift."

Payton nodded. "He's got a point."

"Again," Cole repeated, "I have no idea. For all I know there isn't a fire chief in the state willing to go against the General. Whatever the reason, starting tomorrow, like it or not, I'll be taking my vacation in Hart Land."

"Do you get to bring a guest?" An impish grin teased at one side of Payton's mouth. "A week on the water with a hot date could have its advantages."

"Dude, the guy is going on the invite of a retired United States Marine Corps general." Derrick waved a wooden spoon in Cole's direction. "I don't think the General's looking for the guy to turn the cabin into party city."

The sly grin slipped from Payton's face.

Like Cole had said before, he was about to spend a long week of restful solitude on the lake, whether he liked it or not.

CHAPTER TWO

Sometimes Lily wondered if she shouldn't have become something more nocturnal. Like a nightclub singer, or a late night DJ. Instead, unless she moved to Alaska, she'd fallen in love with the career that required her rising daily long before the sun. Not that chief baker at the Hilltop Inn wasn't everything a local girl could want, but most local girls hadn't studied in France. With her own bakery, Lily could reach so many more people. Of course, even with her own business, sleeping in would never be an option. Fortunately, she could practically bake in her sleep. A little of this, a little of that, extra butter, and voila.

Once she'd finally gotten to sleep last night—correction, earlier this morning—the initial uneasiness that had set in at learning about Margaret's retirement plans had given way to the enthusiasm that Violet had exuded. If she could somehow come up with a way to pull this miracle off, at least she could count on the Hilltop Inn for her first client.

"Purse, keys, coffee," she mumbled to herself. "Looks like I'm all set." Maybe one of these days she'd talk her mother into letting her get a cat. Then she could at least pretend she was talking to someone else and not herself while she got ready in the mornings.

A burst of cool air smacked her at the opening of the front door. Pulling her jacket tightly closed, she had no choice but to admit that the recent tease of warm fall weather had come and gone, and now it was just plain cold.

Hurrying up the path, she fumbled with the key, unlocking the car door the old-fashioned way. No sense in risking waking up a light-sleeping neighbor with a beeping key fob. Her handbag on the passenger seat, her safety belt latched, she paused for a nice long sip of coffee then started the engine. The night air was just cold enough that she indulged in another long swallow before shifting into first gear.

There were lots of things about people she really didn't get, and the love of automatic transmission was one of them. She adored her old Honda. The engine had 10 years of miles on her, used way less gasoline than the guzzlers her sisters drove, but the piece de resistance, the manual transmission was its own theft prevention system. One of the perks of briefly living in France had been learning to drive a stick shift.

Rolling along onto the gravel road that meandered from one side of the family property to the other, she took another quick sip of coffee before turning onto the slightly wider paved road that led off the Hart land. One hand on the gearshift, steering the wheel with her knee, Lily took another swallow of coffee in hopes she might actually feel human by the time she got to the Inn.

Reaching the main drag that cut over the creek and across the small town of Lawford, she set the travel mug down, looked left for any oncoming traffic—not that there was ever anyone on the road at this hour of the morning—and spun the wheel around to the left and picked up speed. Barely into the turn, her headlights flashed on a tall animal in motion.

Her left foot shoved the clutch into the floorboard at the same moment she threw the stick into neutral and slammed on the brakes so hard the rear of the small car heaved up high. Before she could catch her breath or slow her racing heart, what was clearly not an animal but a two-legged man rolled over her hood.

"Oh, God." She'd hit a person. A man. With her car. "Oh, God."

Opening the door, Lily flew from the driver's seat to the other side of the vehicle where the man lay sprawled on a patch of grass—still as stone. "Oh, no." Where was her cousin Heather the doctor when she needed her? Or Cindy. The guy wasn't a pet but at least as a veterinarian Cindy knew more about trauma treatment than she did. Lily sucked in a breath and moved closer. This was no time to panic. Placing two fingers on his neck, she blew out a relieved breath at the steady pulse under her fingertips. "Hospital." She needed to call for help. Except her phone was in her handbag on the passenger seat. Turning on her heel, she glanced at her car. Or where her car should have been. "Oh, no!"

Already on Ralph's neighboring property, the car was rolling down hill and picking up speed. "No," she muttered, running full speed after the old car. She'd left it in neutral without the parking brake. Focused on retrieving her phone and getting help, she didn't see the root sticking up and went flying, arms wide, landing face down with a thud at the exact moment her car slammed into the old neighbor's shed. Someday she'd have to thank her grandfather's friend for not tearing that dilapidated piece of garbage down when the General had asked him to, or her car would now be dangling in the creek.

Ignoring the scrapes on her arms, she scrambled to her feet, flung the door open, grabbed her phone and tore back up the hill. Tapping the familiar numbers nine one one, her mind replayed the body tumbling over her hood in slow motion. What in the name of all that was holy was a good looking guy—yeah, she'd noticed in the seconds it took to find his pulse—doing running in the middle of the street in the middle of the dang night?

● ● ● ●

Daring to open his eyes, Cole blinked up at the stars. The pain shooting up his right shoulder competed with the throbbing in his leg. More precisely, his ankle. Blinking again, he debated if sitting up would be a good idea. Somehow lying still seemed to be leaving all other options behind in the dust. At least until he could unscramble his brain enough to remember why he was lying on the ground, in pain, staring at the stars.

"Yes, Fred. I didn't do it on purpose, hurry." Panic laced the pretty voice. "Oh, his eyes are open!"

Preparing himself for more pain, Cole dared to turn his head in the direction the voice had come from.

"Are you all right?" On her knees, she dropped her phone at her side and ran gentle fingers along his shoulder and down his arm. The one that didn't hurt and was now tingling under her touch.

He blinked. Long red locks hung down in front of his face as she narrowed her eyes in concentration.

"Follow my finger." If he wasn't in so much pain he would have smiled at the intensity with which her orders were given.

A slender finger with trimmed nails and no polish moved from one side of his face to the other.

"Oh, good." Her breath blew low and warm on his face.

Clearly she was pleased with his ability to follow her commands. A nurse or doctor maybe.

The frown deepened. "Where does it hurt?"

Where does it hurt? It would have made more sense to ask where does it *not* hurt. Wiggling the fingers on his left hand, he determined all was well enough, but the movement on his right side had him wishing for a bullet to bite on. *Not good.*

"Lie still. An ambulance is on the way."

"All I need is a few more minutes." He sucked in a deep breath, and using the arm that he was positive didn't hurt, shoved himself to a sitting position. A good soak in a warm tub and an ace bandage was all he needed. He flexed his right hand and swallowed a grimace. Or maybe not.

Even in the dark predawn hours he could see bright green eyes round with worry. "I don't think you should move. I could have, I mean, maybe, I mean… you could be seriously hurt."

Now that he was at her level, he was positive fear and concern were tumbling about behind those eyes. "What happened?"

"You don't remember?" Her brows dipped into a sharp V. "Oh, dear."

Blinking hard, he fought the fog clouding his thoughts. "I went for a run."

"Yes." She blew out a slow breath. "You ran out in front of my car."

Now the pieces were falling into place. He might be on vacation, but his internal clock thought it was another work day and had him wide awake long before the crack of dawn. He'd opted to follow his regular routine of an early morning jog. Except his normal run didn't include colliding with a two thousand pound hunk of metal-in-motion. Quick reflexes had him practically vaulting over the hood to avoid injury, but the effort didn't go as planned. Especially not if the pain on his right side was any indication.

Sirens whirred in the distance, growing louder. Great. Just what he didn't want, to be peeled off the asphalt by one of his EMT buddies and razzed for the rest of his life about losing a match with a... He looked around. "Where's the car?"

"Oh, um." A not-so-steady hand pointed down the hill. "Over there."

Leaning forward for a better view, he cocked an eye. "Where'd you say you got your license?"

Those bright green eyes rolled heavenward and he bit back the urge to smile and tease some more.

"I'll be fine. Help me up." He waved his good arm at her.

Fisted hands came to rest on her hips, elbows sticking out like chicken wings, and a fire in her eyes. They really were very expressive eyes. "Absolutely not. You could have serious injuries. If you would please just wait—"

More words weren't necessary. The ambulance came speeding over the hill, sirens blaring.

"They're here." Relief took over her face.

Doors flew open and two guys in standard uniform stepped out of the vehicle, one coming to a stop beside him. "Well, fancy meeting you here."

The reason Cole was in this mess blinked up at the six-foot former all-star famed for what the women in his department called bedroom eyes. "You two know each other?"

"Work together," Jason answered.

As Cole had expected, he knew the EMT crew. In a county this small, all the emergency services and first responders knew each other both on and off the job. The only way he'd have escaped being the butt of the joke would have been for them to find him bleeding in pieces on the ground. "I'm a firefighter," Cole replied.

"You two don't know each other?" Bryce, the second EMT already assessing Cole's injuries, waved at the woman looking down at them.

The redhead shook her head. "I hit him."

Jason nodded, checking Cole's vitals. "So it seems."

"I'm fine. Twisted my ankle. Maybe dislocated a shoulder."

Bryce looked up from immobilizing the ankle. "No maybe about that shoulder. We'll let the doc get that back in place. Your real problem is the wrist."

Looking down at his right hand, Cole noticed the wrist that was perfectly fine not long ago was twice its normal size. *Crud.*

Gritting his teeth, he turned to face the woman who had carelessly almost mowed him over, only to see all the color drain from her face. "I'm so sorry," she muttered, eyes gleaming with guilt.

He liked the fire in her gaze better. Cutting her some slack was probably in order. After all, it wasn't every day a person slammed into a pedestrian in the middle of the night in the middle of nowhere. He doubted she'd woken up this morning and decided to run down an unsuspecting jogger. On the other hand, it wasn't every day that he got nearly run over by a beautiful woman with eyes the color of a newly sprouted shamrock. All he had to decide now was if that was a good or bad thing.

CHAPTER THREE

I t had taken both EMTs a good fifteen minutes of arguing, and a failed attempt to stand on his own two feet before the man she now knew was named Cole agreed to be transported to the hospital. She'd taken advantage of the few minutes to shoot her boss a text explaining she'd had a little mishap with her car and would not be available this morning. Fortunately, the Inn always kept an emergency stash of frozen baked goods for just such a morning.

"That wrist is going to have you out for at least six weeks," Jason announced.

Cole merely groaned and Lily leaned back a little further in the ambulance. Maybe she should have woken one of her sisters and asked for a ride. Her presence didn't seem to be helping the patient any.

The teasing tone when the EMT driver had smiled at Cole and announced, "Wives and girlfriends are allowed to ride in the bus," told Lily she'd only been allowed along so the guys could taunt him.

Cole had bit down on his back teeth so hard she was afraid he might break a tooth. Not wanting to make things worse—though she didn't know how she possibly could—she opted to keep her mouth shut the entire ride. The way the two men joked and teased went a long way toward minimizing her concerns that the man she'd hit might be more seriously injured.

"Here we are." Jason pushed the doors open.

Waiting her turn, she followed the group, surprised when her phone sounded. She didn't even bother to look at caller ID. It had to be Barb her boss checking up on her. After all, who else would be up at this hour of the morning?

"What in blue blazes is going on?" The General's voice boomed so loudly both EMTs turned to look at her.

Wincing at the sound, she smiled at the men and flashed a thumbs up. Stepping aside, she leaned against the wall and turned her back to the big room. "Good morning, General."

"Might've been if I hadn't strolled outside to see your car kissing Ralph's old shed. Since you were nowhere in sight and are answering your phone, am I to presume you are all right?" Despite the stern tone and harsh words, she could hear the concern seeping through.

"I wasn't in the car when it rolled down the hill."

"Young lady," concern shifted to frustration, "the parking brake is there for a reason."

"Yes sir, I know, sir." Now all she had to decide was how much she wanted to share with the old man. Starting out with "I'm at the hospital" wasn't the best idea. "I accidentally ran over your new guest wasn't much better," but he'd have to find out sooner or later. "I sort of had a little incident at the top of the hill and I got distracted."

"What happened and where in blue blazes are you now?"

Lily swallowed hard. "A jogger, your new guest, the fireman, was hurt—just a little—in a small accident, and I came with him to the hospital."

"Hospital," his voice boomed again. "How small?"

"The EMTs say probably just a sprain, possible dislocated shoulder, and fractured or broken wrist."

Silence lingered a little too long. "Lily Nelson, what was your part in this?"

Sucking in a calming breath, squeezing the phone a little tighter, and focusing on a crack in the ceiling, she muttered, "I sort of hit him with my car."

Her grandfather's exasperated breath sounded moments before he spoke, "Lily, sweetie, there are easier ways to reel in a man."

"I am not trying to reel him in." Her voice went up just enough for the nurse at the station to look up at her with a raised eyebrow. Lily shrugged an apology, smiled and, turning away from the desk, leaned into the phone. She lowered her voice. "It was an accident. What normal person is jogging at 4 o'clock in the morning in the dark in the middle of nowhere?" She sighed. "Never mind. Let me find out how bad it is and then I'll give you a call. We're going to need a ride back to the lake."

"Ten four. Don't you worry, I'll have reinforcements at the ready."

"Sir—" About to ask him to please not do anything till she knew more, she heard the line disconnect. Looking away from the wall, Lily realized she was actually in the ER, not the waiting area. It hadn't occurred to her that the ambulances used a different entrance than the walk-ins. Despite living her entire life in Lawford, this was the first time she'd set foot in the ER. So distracted by the General's call, she hadn't noticed which way the EMTs had gone and didn't have any idea how to find her way out.

"Excuse me," she asked the nurse behind the counter at the same moment a curtain swished open and the two EMTs came toward her, pushing their collapsible gurney and laughing.

"You came in with the hit and run?" the nurse asked her.

"No run. Just hit."

"Yes. Well." The nurse glanced at her screen and back, her chin jutting out toward the cubicle Jason and Bryce had come from. "Your husband's being taken to x-ray as we speak."

"Oh, no. You've misunderstood. He's not my—"

"You behave yourself," Jason called to Cole being pushed away in a wheelchair, and reaching the nurse's station, tapped his ring on the counter. "We have to get going. Don't let the hotshot give you any trouble."

"We can handle him." The nurse smiled brightly and turned to Lily. "You can go with him, or if you'd like you can wait for him in the cubicle. There's no one else in x-ray at the moment, he shouldn't be long."

"Thank you." Lily considered trying once again to explain that she wasn't married, engaged, or in any way involved with the injured party, but decided sometimes, as Lucy would say, *you with your little mouth closed look very pretty.*

● ● ● ●

At least the hammer banging on his brain had slowed to a tolerable tapping.

"So, who won? You or the other guy?" The orderly leaned over Cole's shoulder, steering him toward the elevators.

"Considering the other guy outweighed me by a couple of tons,

I'd say I did."

The brawny orderly who had escorted him back to the ER smiled. "Got to love it when the underdog comes out ahead."

Cole was considering how to respond when the double doors opened automatically and he could see the redhead sitting in his cubicle. He let out a groan.

"What?" The orderly followed the direction Cole's gaze and chuckled. "Since the Mrs. doesn't look to weigh in at one ton, never mind two, and is—no offense—easy on the eyes, you should be grinning from ear to ear, not grumbling."

There was no arguing, the woman was most definitely very easy on the eyes. Not so much the gas pedal. "She's not my Mrs."

"Too bad." The orderly tsked.

What Cole wanted to know was why the woman was still here. She wasn't family, and yes it was her fault he was in the hospital in the first place, but only relatives were supposed to be allowed this deep in the ER. Before he could voice a response either way, the redhead spotted him and sprang to her feet.

"Any more news?" she asked.

Clearly he'd been more rattled than he'd thought this morning. This was one gorgeous woman. Yes, he'd noticed her eyes before, but not much more. Now, standing in front of him, she somehow managed to make an ordinary pair of black slacks and a bland button-down white shirt look anything but ordinary. Long red hair framed her face perfectly. Heart-shaped lips begged to be kissed. *Kissed*? And wasn't he insane for taking inventory and letting his mind run off in any direction. Perhaps he'd hit his head harder than he'd thought.

"The doctor should be back shortly to give you an update." The orderly maneuvered the wheelchair beside the bed. "Need help?"

Cole shot him a glare and gave his daily exercising routine a silent fist pump for allowing him to lift from the chair on one leg without the slightest wobble. Silently sending a told-you-so look of triumph to the orderly, Cole waited for the man to leave before attempting another move. Too bad his moment of accomplishment vanished with his next breath. The second he pushed on his wrist to heft himself onto the bed, a stabbing pain shot up his arm, across his shoulder, and came out his mouth in an audible hiss.

"Oh no." The redhead sprang from her seat and practically catapulted over the bed to his side, making herself at home under his arm. "You should have let the man help you. Lean on me."

At six foot and two hundred pounds of mostly muscle, he almost laughed at her valiant effort. The top of her pretty red head barely reached his shoulder.

"Come on. I'm stronger than I look." She pressed herself closer to him, and for an absurd moment, Cole thought too bad the invitation wasn't to a bigger bed and for a totally different reason.

"I can do this. I just have to use my other hand." Twisting in place, he shimmied away from her and lining his back with the bed, lifted himself onto the high mattress with his good hand and proceeded to bump his bad ankle into the bedside tray contraption. At least he managed to bite back the curse that came to mind.

Hands fisted on her waist, the reason he was in this mess at all shook her head at him. "Stubborn, aren't you?"

Between the once again thundering headache and the pain radiating up and down his body, he didn't have the strength to hold his own head up, never mind debate the difference between self sufficiency and stubbornness.

The curtain swung open and the nurse who had evaluated him on arrival smiled at him. "Your guardian angel was most definitely working overtime."

One could argue if the angel had been on the job, he wouldn't have gotten hit at all, but he wasn't stupid. He'd seen more than his share of victims on the wrong side of an auto collision. At least he was still here to talk about it. A bit worse for wear, but here.

The nurse scrambled to help him elevate his leg. A grumble, groan, and grunt from him later, and she had him all set up. "That wasn't very hard, was it?"

Whether she meant the x-ray, climbing onto the bed, or having his leg propped up in the air like a side of beef, he didn't have a clue. Again, he bit back the words that had sprung to mind.

"The doctor will be here momentarily—"

"The doctor is here now." A tall guy who reminded Cole of that Dreamy character from his ex's favorite TV show flashed the nurse a teasing grin before turning his attention to Cole. "I'm Doctor Gavez, and you are looking pretty good for a man who collided with a moving vehicle."

"Then the wrist isn't broken?"

"Oh, no." Dr. Gavez gave a shake of his head. "It's definitely broken."

"And the ankle?" It would be bad enough that a broken wrist was going to keep him off the job for at least six weeks, the last thing he needed to add to it was only one good leg for just as long.

"There you got off lucky. Only a sprain."

Somehow that didn't sound very lucky to him. Even a simple sprain required rest and elevation. With a broken wrist he could go back to work right away on light desk duty. He would have hated it, but at least he wouldn't be lying around counting the cracks on the ceiling.

"We'll get a cast on that wrist then set you up with a pair of crutches."

Cole wished he'd had a camera to take a picture of the look on the redhead's face. If her eyebrows had shot any higher on her forehead, they'd brush her hair.

"Yes," the doctor said with an air of frustration. "It's a bit of an oxymoron to send a patient with a cast on his arm home with crutches they clearly can't use. Unfortunately, there's no back up for sending you home with something more suitable for a broken wrist."

Her eyes back in her head, Lily nodded. "Not a problem. I'm pretty sure we still have a wheelchair in the attic that we used when my Great Granny couldn't use a walker anymore."

Great Granny? "It's a sprain," Cole repeated.

"That you need to rest and elevate for at least a week. Depending on swelling and bruising, possibly two," the doctor responded.

"I'll phone ahead to Hart House and have someone get the chair out of the attic." Lily bobbed her head as if reassuring herself it was all settled. "Fortunately, all the cabins are ramp accessible."

"Wait a minute," Cole interrupted. He wasn't going back to the cabin. Well, maybe just long enough to pack up and go home, but that was it. "I'm not staying at the cabin as planned."

"Why not?" The disgruntled pinch between her brows actually looked cute.

"If I'm going to be laid up I'd rather it be in my own apartment. Besides…" Thoughts scrambled in search of a better reply. Nothing clawed its way to the surface. Regardless of where the roof over his head was, he couldn't use crutches, couldn't walk, and the desperate longing for a good hot shower that would have to wait a good long while reminded him nothing about the next week or two would be easy.

"I do have another concern," the doctor interrupted. "The tests don't show any serious head injury—"

"Head injury?" All the color—not for the first time this morning—drained from the pretty redhead's face.

"But you'll need to be monitored for the appearance of more serious symptoms. I can't discharge you unless there's someone to keep an eye on you."

Lily nodded. "How long?"

"At least tonight. Another day wouldn't hurt."

This time the woman bobbed her head once in definitive move that shouted there was no room for disagreement. "Then it's settled," she said. "You can't be alone. I'd better go wait for our ride home in the visitor's lounge until you're ready to be released. Unless," she glanced at the doctor, "I'm needed here for something more?"

The doctor shook his head. "It's pretty slow this morning. You go on. We'll have his wrist set quickly, then we can go over what you'll need to be looking for."

"Great." For the first time all night, she smiled. Really smiled. Her cheeks pinkened, her eyes twinkled, and lifting at the corners, her lips parted slightly. For a fraction of a minute he was actually glad she'd hit him before the insanity of that ridiculous thought struck him. Whatever meds they'd given him, they weren't going to be strong enough to help him survive a night with a much too cheerful redhead.

CHAPTER FOUR

"Tesiahere you are." Violet eased her way out of the wobbly orange vinyl seat in the waiting room. "The General was going to come himself but I volunteered."

"Thank you. I'm not sure I'm steady enough to face our grandfather just yet."

"How is he? Attila the Hun over there won't give me an update."

Lily gave her cousin a tight squeeze, drawing strength from the woman she loved as much as her own sisters. "You should have texted me."

"I almost did, then I decided if you needed me, you'd call me." Violet eased back from the embrace. "What's the prognosis?"

"Broken wrist and sprained ankle. Doctor put his shoulder back in place."

"That's it?"

Lily nodded. "Isn't that enough?"

"Lucy says he's a looker."

Well, Lily couldn't very well disagree. She'd practically found herself drooling when she finally got a good look at him. The guy could be on the cover of any romance novel he wanted. "I'm more worried about the fact that I could have killed him."

"Oh, honey." Violet flung her arms around her younger cousin again. "I'm so sorry."

For a long minute Lily took solace in another embrace. She didn't think she'd ever known terror before this morning. Now there was no doubt.

"Do we have a plan?" Violet asked.

Lily pulled back and sighed. "Other than looking for Granny's old wheelchair? No." And that was the truth. She'd put on a lot of bravado back there about taking care of him, but the reality was she had hadn't been able to think any further than finding the blasted wheelchair.

"Maybe one of those scooter things would be better?"

"Scooter?"

"You know, that thing that lets you rest your knee on a ledge and then roll around using mostly your good foot. It's designed for two hands, but I'm sure the big strong fireman can manage with one."

Lily knew her cousin was teasing, but she could still feel the heat rising to her cheeks at just how big and strong the guy felt at her side. The double doors opened to the waiting room and the same orderly wheeled Cole through. One arm in a sling for his shoulder, his wrist and ankle taken care of, the man didn't look any happier about coming to Hart House than he had a short while ago.

The doctor followed behind Cole's wheelchair and came to a stop beside Lily and her cousin. Introductions were made all around, then he gave Lily the papers he held in his hand. "These are instructions for care after a head injury."

"I don't have a head injury." Cole raised his casted wrist.

"You're a fireman. You should know the routine as well as the rest of us. The information is self-explanatory. If you have any questions, feel free to call. I wrote my cell number on the bottom."

"Thank you."

"Very well." The doctor hesitated a moment and turned to Cole. Patting his shoulder, he said, "Don't give the lady a hard time," before strolling back through the double doors.

Her gaze on the closed doors, Violet mumbled, "That man can give me a hard time whenever he wants."

"Violet!" Lily elbowed her cousin in the ribcage, pretending not to notice the chuckle Cole failed to smother.

"What?" she snapped back.

Rolling her eyes, Lily shook her head and waved the orderly on. "Let's get home."

"Did you at least notice if he was single?" Lowering her voice, Violet fell into step beside her cousin.

"No," Lily muttered through clenched teeth. "I had more important things on my mind." Like explaining to her grandfather that not only had she almost killed a guest, but the man's week long stay might very well be a bit longer. And at the Hart House expense.

"You two wait here. I'll bring my car to the curb." Slipping around the wheelchair, Violet hurried through the hospital doors.

Lily nodded. Butterflies were flapping around in her stomach like angry geese and it had nothing to do with whether or not the handsome doctor was single. Contrary to what her cousin Violet might think, having a drop dead gorgeous patient to care for scared her even more than having almost killed the man.

• • • •

"Sorry about the bumps." Violet slowed to a stop in front of Cole's cottage and shoved the gearshift into park. "I never noticed how bumpy the access road is."

"No problem." Cole managed the closest thing to a reassuring smile he could muster, considering most of his body throbbed like hell regardless of the pot holes in the road.

Lily hopped out of the passenger side and flung his car door open. "Give me a second to get the scooter out of the trunk."

"Should we call the General and let him know we're back?" Violet skirted the hood and met her cousin at the rear of the car.

"Let's get him settled first."

"If you say so, but…"

Enough was enough. He was neither a cranky baby nor spastic puppy in need of 'settling' in. Careful to ease his bad foot out the door, he carefully used his good arm to help leverage himself up and onto his uninjured foot. "I've got this, ladies."

Two heads whipped around. The scooter on the ground, Lily actually rolled her eyes like a petulant teen. "You're going to be difficult, aren't you?"

"I'm not the one who insisted on getting this contraption."

"It was this," she nudged the scooter closer to where he stood, "or Granny's wheelchair. Even though I have concerns about you overusing that shoulder, you already made it clear you didn't want the wheelchair."

She had him there. He'd been rather vocal about his dislike of the whole idea.

"Let's see how this works for you." She set the contraption in front of him.

Close enough that he barely had to shift his weight to rest the knee of his newly injured leg onto the lone cushioned knee rest. Gripping the handle bar one handed, he took in the short length of the front walkway. He didn't remember it seeming so long when he'd checked in yesterday. Of course, nothing seemed like it had yesterday. "Forward ho."

"Are you sure? Maybe I should help—" The look on his face was enough to stutter her next words. "Yes, sir."

Violet scurried ahead to open the door and Lily inched along beside him, her one hand hovering near him like a new mother protecting her toddler while taking his first steps. So far, so good. The walkway was level ground, making steering the scooter with one arm fairly easy. Even crossing the threshold hadn't posed much of a challenge. Yet, by the time he'd made it from one end of the tiny cabin's living area to the other, he'd collapsed onto the sofa like a man who had just finished a triathlon.

Satisfied he wasn't about to spring up from the couch and bolt out the door on her, she waved a hand at him. "I'll get some pillows from the bedroom."

"That won't be—"

The wave of an arm and her disappearing back silenced him.

"Here we go." She scurried back from the hall in his direction. "Leg up."

He considered insisting he could do this himself, but not only was he exhausted from the entire ordeal, after only a few hours together he was already beginning to recognize the look in her eye. The one that clearly announced she was not going to back down. Lifting his leg high enough for her to gently shove a few pillows in place for support, he bit back a smile. And the woman called *him* stubborn.

"Is it time to call the General yet?" Violet came from the kitchen, a glass of water in one hand.

"I suppose I'll have to face the music."

"How bad can it be?" Lily rolled her eyes and immediately Violet waved her hand. "Forget I said that."

"Ladies." Until now Cole didn't realize how much he disliked people talking about him as if he wasn't in the room. "It's been a long morning. Why don't you both go home and I'll just turn on the TV, maybe take a nap."

"Oh, no." Lily spun around shaking her head. "No naps just yet and I can't leave you alone."

Before he could muster an argument, the front door flung open. A sturdy woman waltzed into the house, holding a stack of pillows. Without pausing, she continued straight to the bedroom. "General is right behind me."

He wasn't sure if her words were a report or a warning. Not two seconds later, two golden retrievers announced the arrival of the General. The dogs had never left the man's side the entire time Cole had been inspecting the smoke alarms, and he was a little surprised to see them abandon their master to come sit at his side. One dog sniffed at his feet while the other took in his broken wrist and sniffed at his temple, leaned away and then sniffed again. If he didn't know better he'd have sworn the animal was frowning.

"It's okay, girl," he whispered. "Just a little headache."

Apparently, he hadn't whispered low enough. From a few feet away, Violet heard his quiet confession. "I have just the thing for that. Be right back."

"And where are you off to?" The General blocked Violet's path.

"I'll be right back. Just getting something for his headache." Pausing to kiss her grandfather on the cheek, she spun around him smiling and dashed out the door and up the walkway.

"Really," the General huffed.

The older woman came back down the hall. "I put extra pillows in the closet. Let me know if you need anything more. Also have a pot of chicken soup started at the house. Best medicine for whatever ails you."

"Good idea, Lucy." The General nodded. "Thank you."

"Have to keep the young man's strength up." Nodding at the General, Lucy turned to Cole and smiled. "You take it easy. That foot's going to need lots of rest."

For some reason, Cole felt the need to come to attention but settled for a nod and a quiet "thank you."

Lucy gave a curt dip of her chin then spun around and marched out the door much the way she'd come in.

"Now," the General took a seat, "what exactly did the doctor say?"

"RICE. Rest, ice, compression, elevation," Lily answered for him. "Which is why I've already called Barb and told her I'll be baking here for the next few mornings instead of at the Inn."

"Here?" The General's brows lifted high on his forehead.

"Here we go." Violet bounced into the room waving her hands in the air. It took Cole a moment to realize she held a vial in each hand. "Lavender and Peppermint."

"Violet." Lily frowned.

"Don't worry." The cheery brunette eased onto the floor beside him with the grace of a prima ballerina. "Just a few drops on each temple—"

"Wait a second." Fingers splayed wide, Cole waved his good hand at her.

Violet and Lily smiled in unison.

"No worries." Violet held a dropper over him. "This will help with those headaches. Essential oils. They won't hurt, I promise."

"Violet, dear," the General spoke. "If the man doesn't want—"

"General, sir." Lily cleared her throat. "It can't hurt."

"There you go." Before he could object, Violet had squeezed the drops onto his temple and rubbed them gently in. "You should start to feel better soon."

The only way he was going to feel better was if everyone left him alone to catch a few winks.

"All right." Violet sprang to her feet. "I hate to heal and run, but I've got a yoga for seniors' class Grams organized starting in twenty minutes."

"Thanks," Lily called to her.

"Any time, cuz."

Cuz. The two seemed so close, Cole had assumed they were sisters.

A soft rap sounded on the door.

"Yoo hoo." A lovely woman with shoulder length white hair and bright blue eyes seemed to float into the room. "How is our patient doing?"

"Fine, ma'am. Thank you." He wasn't really, but something

about the gentle manner of his newest visitor made him think so.

"That's good. I'm Fiona Hart. Our Lily will take good care of you." The woman studied him momentarily before smiling and turning to the General. "Katie phoned. She found her grandmother's set of fine crochet hooks from Ireland for me to try. Shall I ask George to give me a lift to the One Stop?"

The General sprang to his feet with the speed of a new recruit under the watchful eye of his drill sergeant. "George is working on some loose boards on the back porch. I'll drive you."

"Thank you, dear. I'll meet you back at the house." The General's wife turned toward Cole. "Feel better soon." Then she left the room as gracefully as she'd entered.

"Very well." The General faced his granddaughter. "We might as well walk back to the house and let the young man rest."

"No." Lily shook her head. "He can't be left alone."

The General frowned.

"Concussion." She said the single word as though that would explain everything. And judging by the tight press of the old man's mouth, it had. "I'll move my things down here for a couple of days until we're sure he's all right."

"Here?" The General's tone dropped an octave. "Alone?"

Not since he'd been caught making out with the pastor's daughter had a single word made Cole feel completely and totally chastised.

"Yes, here," she said matter of factly, conveniently ignoring the alone comment. "This is his cabin for the week."

Shaking his head, the General seemed to struggle to pry his mouth open and spit out words. "Absolutely not. I will not have my granddaughter cohabitating with a single man."

"General." A soft sigh showed Lily's struggle to hide the exasperation from her voice. "We are not cohabitating. There are two bedrooms, and if you haven't noticed, his injuries leave him at a serious disadvantage for co-anything."

Cole almost objected to the comment and immediately recognized it was not in his best interest to prove to the General that he was not nearly as incapacitated as his granddaughter believed.

"I don't like it." The General shook his head. "Not one bit."

"General." Lily eased over to her grandfather and placed a gentle kiss on his cheek. "Grams is waiting for you at the house. Go on. We'll be fine here. Besides, Lucy will be back soon with some chicken soup and we'll have a proper chaperone."

The last words were obviously said playfully, but he could tell there was enough emphasis to reflect the truth of the statement.

"I don't know," the old man blustered.

Lily nudged him gently toward the door. "I think I hear Grams calling."

If she did, the woman had bionic ears. The main house was most definitely too far up the hill to hear anyone calling.

"Well," the General allowed himself to be ushered a few steps forward, "I'll be back soon. But remember," he stepped over the threshold onto the front path, "no fraternizing amongst the ranks."

Somehow Lily managed to keep a straight face, smile, and ease the front door closed as she nodded. "No fraternization. Got it."

The door fully shut, she spun about and leaned back heavily. "That could have been so much worse."

The events of the last few hours ran through his mind. Hit by a car. A broken wrist. A dislocated shoulder. A sprained ankle. A week off his feet. A beautiful woman to care for him…and… a Marine Corps general standing guard over them. He wasn't at all sure how it could have been any worse.

• • • •

Harold Hart stood momentarily still outside the colorful cabin door and shook his head. Sensible, smart, capable and caring, with a lousy sense of direction and even worse sense of balance. He supposed if any of his granddaughters were to hit a man with her car, it shouldn't surprise him that it would be his Lily.

And now that same man was going to be laid up in his cabin in need of constant supervision for at least the next forty-eight hours.

He shook his head again and followed behind Lady and Sarge toward the main house. "Not at all what I expected. But," a hint of a smile teased at the corners of his mouth as he nodded to himself, "it could work."

CHAPTER FIVE

"Okay." Lily slapped her hands together and rubbed vigorously. She'd talked him into coming back to the cabin. For the first time in her life she'd tossed her grandfather out the door, insisting she needed to be here at the cabin. That left one question. Now what? "Do you need anything?" she asked, hoping for a little direction.

"Nope. I'm all set." Flashing a ridiculously stiff smile, Cole blew out a deep breath and looked left then right, his gaze finally settling on the remote control just outside his reach.

"I'll get that." Lily leaped forward. Tripping over her handbag on the floor, she nearly landed in his lap before catching her balance. Quickly snatching the remote off the table, she handed it to him as though stumbling across the room were perfectly normal.

Leaning on his good hand, Cole's lips tightened.

"Hang on." Lily eased forward, studying the man reclining on the sofa. It was obvious that any movement was jostling the sore shoulder. "We have two choices here."

"We?"

"We. I can come up behind you and try to help you sit up so it doesn't hurt. Or I can bring some extra cushions to prop behind your back instead."

"Or," Cole bit back a smile, "I could just push myself and sit up." He pressed his good hand into the sofa and scooted back. "Like that."

"I've already mentioned you're rather stubborn, haven't I?"

"You have." Pointing the remote at the TV, he searched for a show to watch.

"Hmm." Studying the new elevation of the injured leg, she grabbed a cushion from the nearby chair and stood hovering over his bad leg. "We might need to raise this higher."

"Any higher and I'll be able to receive alien communications that entire satellite systems are incapable of."

A sputtered laugh slipped out. Quickly she covered her mouth and took a step back. So the man did have a sense of humor.

For the first time today, Cole smiled up at her. She had no idea why, but his smile was broad and bright and made his gray eyes sparkle.

"You might need to be perched outdoors for the alien reception thing to actually work. With a tin foil hat." She smothered another giggle. "You know, just for effect."

Cole rolled his eyes but the smile remained intact.

"Are you hungry?"

Pointing the remote at the bulky old TV, he shook his head at the same time his stomach rumbled loudly enough to alert the aliens of his lie.

Lily lifted her brows in a silent re-asking.

"Well." Somehow the twinkle in his already sparkling eyes grew brighter. "Maybe just a little."

"Excellent." She spun around. "Feeding people is something I do well."

"As opposed to?" He put the remote down and heaving out a sigh, leaned back against the pillows.

Staring into the near empty refrigerator she took inventory. Apples, cabbage, spinach, nuts, all the fixings for a decent salad, but nothing for a tasty meal. No bread, no juice, no milk. She opened a few cupboards. No coffee. Didn't the cabins come stocked with basics?

"What are you looking for?"

"Right now, a coffee pot."

"Under the sink." He waved toward the kitchen.

Surely she'd heard him wrong. Opening the lower cabinet, she immediately spotted the old coffee maker. "Why, if you don't mind my asking, is the coffee pot under here?"

"It was in my way."

"You don't drink coffee?" Maybe he really was an alien. After all, every human she'd ever known had been addicted to morning caffeine in some way, whether coffee or tea.

"Nope."

Taking in the countertop again, she realized a blender along with some containers and canisters took up the space where the coffee pot would normally be. The only one she might even slightly consider fit for human consumption was the protein powder.

"I wasn't sure if I'd have one of the cabins with much refrigerator space. I thought I'd hit the store today for some basics."

She bobbed her head, not sure she wanted to know what he considered basics. "If you promise me you will behave yourself, I'm going to run over to the main house a minute and pick up a few things for a decent breakfast."

"I've got some bananas on the counter. I can make a smoothie."

"Smoothie? I don't think so." Shaking her head, she inched her way out of the small kitchen. "I'll be back in a flash."

Cole stared at her just long enough for her to think he was about to argue when he nodded and returned his attention to the remote control.

Quietly closing the door behind her, she trotted up the hill to Hart House. White Victorian with a wraparound porch, the building stood as a testament to the strength and love of the Lawford-Hart family. She only wished that sometimes the family tree didn't come rooted with a stubborn, iron-willed retired general.

"No fraternizing among my troops," she muttered to herself. Really. Only her grandfather could make her feel like a raw recruit.

"Whoa." Arms full, Violet spun around by the kitchen entry, wobbling to regain her balance.

"Well done." Lucy grinned from her spot behind the sink. "You always make almost falling over look so graceful. You know, Louise Franklin told me that her nephew is a very good dancer. Light on his feet. I bet—"

"Lucy," Violet and Lily echoed.

"What?" The woman had the nerve to look up as though she'd been chastised for saving a kitten.

Shaking her head at the woman she loved like family, Lily took a step back and surveyed her cousin's arms. "What's all this?"

"Turns out the General thought that George stocked the fireman's cabin, George thought Grams did it, Grams thought Lucy had, and Lucy thought the General had."

"And that's why the place looks like Mother Hubbard's cupboard?"

"Yep. These are the basics."

"And some of my breakfast casserole. Just pulled it out of the oven," Lucy called over her shoulder.

Violet nodded. "I thought I'd run them by quickly before my class."

"Well good. That's why I'm here. Hand them over and I'll take them back."

"Ah ah." Violet shook her head. "You may have hit him first but I'm calling dibs on the rest of him."

"Girls. Your grandfather will be down any moment to take me to the One Stop to see Katie." In a floral skirt that would make any gypsy proud, their grandmother set her project bag with her latest crafting effort on the counter and moved forward to kiss each granddaughter on the cheek "What have we taught you?"

Violet's shoulders deflated. "No man is worth fighting with family over."

"Except we're not fighting." It may be Lily's responsibility to keep Cole on the mend but she certainly didn't have her eyes set on him for anything else. The last thing she needed in her life now was another self-absorbed good-looking hunk.

"Good." Violet perked up. "Then I'll take these things over."

"That's silly." Lily's voice rose a fraction of an octave in frustration. "He's expecting me to fix him breakfast."

Her grandmother walked past, lightly patting Lily on the arm. "I was a bit concerned when your grandfather told me what happened, but the young man seems to have come out of the unfortunate incident well. All will be fine."

Violet smiled a little too broadly. "You know what they say about lemons into lemonade."

"Mm," Grams hummed, looking at Lily. "Your grandfather says you're going to be staying with the fireman in his cabin."

Her cousin's big blue eyes rounded double in size. "She is?"

"It's not like we're going to be playing house," Lily snapped. "The man needs help."

"Agreed." Violet bobbed her head once. "I volunteer to… help."

"That won't be necessary, dear." Grams smiled that soft smile that came so easily whenever she was about to explain to the girls why, whether it was cake for breakfast or a man in their midst, life just didn't always work the way they wanted. "This young man is Lily's responsibility."

The skin over Violet's perfectly shaped brows folded like a Shar Pei puppy's. Practically pouting, she set the bag in her arms on the island. "How come she gets to keep him?"

"That's easy." Lucy looked up from her spot peeling potatoes over the sink. "She caught him."

"I didn't catch him!" Why did everyone keep saying that to her?

"Okay," Lucy shrugged. "You hit him. Feel better?"

"No." The air puffed out of her lungs. The horror of seeing Cole roll across the hood of her little Honda gave her the chills.

"It's all right, dear." Her grandmother's arm curled around her shoulder.

From her other side, Violet wrapped an arm around her as well. "I'm sorry. Grams is right. You can keep him."

• • • •

Not a blessed thing worth watching on TV. Apparently befitting the concept of family time and leisure living, the television had no cable, only local channels. Now what? All his belongings, including the book he'd brought, were in the bedroom. His gaze landed on the knee scooter in the corner of the room. He could easily hop over and roll into the room and be back with his book and Florence Nightingale wouldn't probably notice, but despite his bravado, everything hurt like hell even with the pain meds, and he had about as much energy as a sloth before a much needed nap. Not to mention he understood too well that even though the doctor had slipped his shoulder back into place, unless he wanted to slip it back out, he needed to let it heal. Tomorrow he could deal with one handed scooter maneuvers. Today, much to his surprise, he was glad to have someone around to help. Just a little.

Which didn't solve the problem of what-to-do-for-distraction until Lily returned. Within reach on the coffee table was the baggie with all his personal effects. The ER attendant had emptied his pockets and one of the two women must have brought them back.

Cell phone in hand, he tapped on his partner's number.

"Payton here."

"And where exactly would here be?"

"Hey man. Didn't expect to hear from you this week. Thought for sure, general or no general, you'd be otherwise occupied."

"Funny. I dare you to stare down the General—and our boss—when he catches you fraternizing."

"What?"

"Nothing. Just something the General said when he left me a little while ago. No fraternizing under his command."

"Was that a warning or did he catch you with the, er, goods?"

"No goods. The only thing I got close and personal with was a compact car."

"What?" Alarm rang in Payton's voice rather than confusion. "Man, you better be pulling my leg."

"Since my right wrist is broken, not likely."

"Okay. What the hell happened?"

"On my morning jog I sort of ran a collision course with a small car." And a pretty redhead.

"The only reason I'm not letting the words jogging and car collision escalate my blood pressure is that you're still here to call me. What hospital are you in?"

Without the man saying a word, Cole could almost hear his buddy dressing and gathering his belongings to race out the door. "I'm not. I've been discharged already." No point in mentioning the part about *with* supervision.

"Then you're okay. Just a broken wrist?"

"And sprained ankle." Why bring up the dislocated shoulder and probable concussion? If he did, his friend would crawl through the phone line.

A heavy groan sounded in his ear. "So what you're telling me is I'm going to be stuck with Regan for the next six weeks until that wrist heals?"

"Sorry." He really was. The last thing he wanted was to be laid up. "As we speak my foot is elevated higher than my heart and I can feel the swelling shrinking away. I'll be up and about sooner than you think."

"Don't push it, man. Remember Dukowski? Set himself back so often he had to have the very surgery he was hoping to avoid."

"I know." And he did. There was a fine line between helpful exercise and overdoing. And for the next seven days, almost everything he wanted qualified as overdoing. From the kitchen window across the cabin he could see the top of Lily's red hair making its way to the door. "Listen. I'm going to catch forty winks. I'll check back in a few days."

"Remember what I said. Don't overdo it."

The call disconnected at the same moment the latch on the front door clicked open. Instinct had him pushing up in his seat to relieve her of the bundles she carried. Pain up his arm and across his back reminded him why Lily was here in the first place.

"Good." She smiled at him. "I was afraid I was going to find you hobbling laps around the place."

"Hardly." Not that the thought hadn't occurred to him. Less than an hour banned to the couch and the sense of entrapment was setting in.

"I've got some of the staples that should have been in the cabin for your arrival and a few extras. Thought I'd whip up a treat to say thank you."

Whatever she had in mind, Cole was willing to bet his career the treat had nothing to do with the first thing that popped into his head. Too bad.

"I'll fry up some bacon and heat up last night's croissants. They already have extra butter but nothing melts in your mouth like a warm croissant with fresh butter."

Cole blinked and almost shook his head in an effort to reset his brain. Why did every word out of this nice, sweet girl's—and he didn't have to spend any more time with her to know Lily was definitely what his mom called a nice girl—why did every word out of her mouth send his imagination in the totally wrong direction. Twenty-four hours alone with her could be the death of him. Maybe if he was lucky all that extra butter would hurry up clogging his arteries and take him out of his impending misery.

CHAPTER SIX

"Another minute and your late breakfast will be ready." Lily flipped the last of the easy-over eggs and then slid them onto a dish. The nice thing about a small cabin was that she could have fun in the kitchen and still keep an eye on Cole reading across the way, or occasionally nodding off. Once or twice she considered going over and tapping him lightly, but before she could muster the nerve to see if he was okay, he'd jerk his eyes open and return to the book. Even in sleep, the man was stubborn. Thank heaven she only had to do battle with him for another day or so.

Cole closed the book and set it aside, rolled his neck left, then right. The next time Lily glanced over, he stared at his right hand, flexing his fingers. From what little she'd seen of this man, she suspected none of this was going to be easy on him. A plate in hand, she painted on a smile and braved her way across the room. "Here you go."

"Thank you." His gaze warily skimmed the plate from the bacon to the eggs to the casserole, before sharing a slim smile.

What was that all about? Most people she knew would light up at a lumberjack breakfast like that. Though she had skipped the flapjacks for Lucy's casserole. "I thought it would be okay if you sat upright just long enough to eat."

He nodded and using his upper body strength more than his good arm, turned to sit in front of the coffee table. For a few awkward moments Lily buzzed around him like a flustered moth to an irresistible flame. She placed pillows on the floor to rest his bad foot on, set up a TV tray in front of him, and arranged the food and drink as if he were a helpless toddler learning to eat.

"It looks… delicious." Holding the fork in mid-air and staring down at the plate, his declaration didn't sound terribly convincing.

"The breakfast casserole is Lucy's favorite. Mostly I consider it baked French toast. That's why I fried some eggs and bacon for protein." The timer sounded and she spun around, scurrying back to the kitchen. There was a fine line between warming the croissants and turning them into chew toys.

"Yo," a deep voice called from the doorway.

Three men, one bigger than the next, marched into the now much smaller space. One man carried a large pizza box, another the size of a linebacker held a six pack in each hand.

"Man, this place smells good." The third man attached to the voice, carried a large sack from the nearby farmer's market and sniffed the air, stopping short when he spotted Lily. "Hello."

The two others spun around to see her standing with the plate of warm croissants.

The tallest of the group, the one with the sack cracked a huge smile and turned to face Cole. "Aren't you a sly one? Payton here made it sound like you were on death's doorstep. He didn't say a word about the angel at the gates."

Cole's brows slanted into an irritated V as his buddy made his way past her into the kitchen and began unloading every leafy green vegetable known to man.

"Are those warm?" The one holding the pizza set the box down on the coffee table.

Lily blinked, her hand going to her face seconds before she realized the man meant the croissants not her cheeks. Which, if they weren't flushed at the sight of three good-looking men suddenly appearing like the genie from Aladdin's lamp, they certainly were now.

"Yes," she muttered quickly. The man nodded and smiled politely, kicking her manners into gear. "Would you like one?"

"I think Cole here needs fuel more than me."

"Oh, I have more in the kitchen. I made a fresh batch last night."

"Made?" The bruiser's eyes rounded. "Like, from scratch?"

Lily couldn't help the grin that tugged at the corners of her mouth. She loved it when people appreciated her food. "Yes. From scratch."

Hurrying, she set the plate down in front of Cole and went back to the kitchen. It only took a moment to pile the remaining warm croissants on another dish and present them to the three men hovering in the middle of the room. One by one they reached for the flaky French breads.

"Oh, man."

"These are great."

"If this is the reward for getting hit by a car, line me up."

Lily had no idea whether to puff up at the compliment or whither at the reminder she could have killed Cole.

"That's enough, guys." Cole sounded like a big brother reminding the younger family members to mind their manners.

"Why? Because we like real food instead of salads?" The tall one spun around to face her. Holding the half-eaten croissant in one hand, he got down on bended knee and reached for her hand with the other. "Will you marry me?"

Lily giggled. She actually giggled.

"Maybe," Cole's tone dripped with irritation, "I should introduce you first."

His buddy stood. "Good idea. I'm Gabe. I work with this guy at the department."

"Lily Nelson. Nice to meet you."

"Same here. Now that you know my name and that I'm gainfully employed, Lily, will you marry me?"

"If you don't want him," the Bruiser interrupted, flashing a blinding smile, "I'm Payton and available."

The pizza man stuck his hand out. "I'm Regan."

"What?" Gingerly, Cole leaned back against the sofa and skewered Pizza Man with a sharp glare. "Aren't you going to propose too?"

Regan leaned over and grabbing Cole's fork, stabbed at the casserole, then took a big bite, moaned, and turned to her. "Did you bake this too?"

"No." Lily shook her head. "Lucy made that."

"It will be a hard choice," Regan teased, "but I may have to save myself for Lucy."

Cole snatched the fork away from his buddy seconds before an attractive blonde came through the front door, a small carryon in hand. Her gaze darted from man to man, finally settling on Lily. "I, uh, came by the house to check on another stray Grams has been feeding and Lucy asked me to bring you this. Said you needed a few things for over...night." Her voice faltered on the last words as she considered the situation.

"Oh, you have been holding out on us." Teasing, Gabe turned to Cole.

Lily bit back a smile. "This is my sister Hyacinth, better known to all as Cindy."

Immediately, the three men extended a hand and introduced themselves.

Regan's smile lit up his face, and most likely left a trail of broken hearts in its wake. "I don't suppose you cook too?"

Another charmer. Lily had to wonder if a heart-stopping smile was part of the job description for the county fire department.

Still stunned at all the testosterone in the room, Cindy shook her head. While Lily was at home in the kitchen, Cindy had always had a gift with animals. Big ones, little ones, males, females, and from the flutter of activity in the small cabin, clearly males of the human variety, too.

"Didn't you just get engaged?" Cole snapped at his friend.

"She hasn't said yes," Gabe shot back, before facing Lily. "Have you?"

Lily couldn't help the laughter that bubbled loudly to the surface. This entire scenario was absolutely absurd and totally delightful. "Sorry, but I think we should get to know each other more. I mean, you might really hate my crème brulee and then where would we be?"

"Oh, man. She's killing me." Gabe rolled his eyes. "I love crème brulee."

Shaking her head and almost smiling, Cindy looked from Lily to the man on the sofa, to the three guys settling down around the room. "So what you're all saying is the way to a man's heart truly is through his stomach?"

Lily noticed the delighted nods from at least three of the guys in the room and for the first time, really believed maybe loving to bake hadn't been such a bad career choice after all.

● ● ● ●

Cole loved the guys he worked with. All of them. Even the ones who annoyed the crap out him. They were brothers in a way most people wouldn't understand. But watching them shovel down food as though they hadn't been fed in a month and listening to them tease and flirt with Lily and her sister had gotten on his last nerve.

"Wow." The door clicked shut and leaning against it much the way she had earlier in the day after her grandfather's visit, Lily blew a burst of air at a wisp of hair hanging in front of her face. "Are they like that all the time?"

"Like what?"

"For one thing—hungry. Payton downed breakfast and half the pizza."

He shrugged. All of them could pack away the fuel. A serious fire could take hours to put out and there was no room for fatigue. "Sometimes."

"So the energy level goes with it?" She collapsed on the seat across from him.

Energy? He hadn't noticed that. All he'd noticed was that each of them had been in Casanova mode. "Maybe."

Head resting on the chair back, eyes closed, all the tension of the morning had slid away from her features. *Angel at the gates*. Gabe had gotten that much right. Any artist would love to have Lily for a model. It struck him as oddly amusing to realize that in baggy pants, a high collared button-down shirt, and less than fashionable work shoes, she still looked beautiful. When he thought about all the hours his ex spent in front of a mirror and the money squandered on trendy clothes, for the first time he felt sorry for his ex. She could have primped and preened from now till the second coming and she would never have looked as captivating as Lily did sleeping on a chair in her work clothes. He also couldn't imagine his ex putting her personal life aside for even ten minutes to take care of a stranger, regardless of if she'd run him over half a dozen times.

Battling the weight of his own exhaustion, Cole blinked a time or two before finally giving in and letting his eyes drift shut for a moment of rest. He'd gladly sleep a week if his pretty hostess would let him. Most likely, if he dared catch forty winks, Lily would probably spring up at his first snore. Prying his heavy lids open, he reminded himself he only wanted to rest a minute. Or two. Or more.

The next time he forced his eyes open, he knew he'd been asleep for longer than intended. Not only did the large clock on his cell phone screen keep him abreast of the almost hour that had passed, but the persistent tingle along his right forearm was teetering on a full-blown irritation.

Not till he'd rubbed the casted arm for a few minutes with his good hand did he realize the irritation was an outright itch. And not a simple accessible itch. No, he had to have an inch starting at the edge of his wrist and working its way up and away from the cast. Cast being the operative word. Because of the swelling, the snug fit didn't allow enough space to slip a finger down, even if his were a slim six inches long. Which they weren't.

Scratching at the exposed flesh was doing nothing to relieve the growing discomfort. Scanning the coffee tabletop, he looked for something within reach that would do the trick. A letter opener would be great. A knife would do. Hell, he'd settle for a nail file or ice pick.

"Stop that." The sound came from across the room.

Her eyes still closed, and her body in the same relaxed position she'd been in for nearly an hour, he almost believed he'd imagined the words.

"I said, stop that." Lily pulled herself up in the chair, rubbed the sleep from her eyes, then ran her hands loosely through her hair. "I can hear you scratching all the way over here."

"It's itchy." Though obvious, it was a safer response than stuttering, even with your hair sticking out in every direction, you look amazing.

She pushed to her feet. "Ignore it."

"Easier said than done."

"I have faith in you." Flashing a sleepy smile, she stretched her back and took a step forward. "Since I'm not going to the Inn today, I'm going to change into something more comfortable."

Once again, his mind meandered down a path it had no business taking. Maybe it was the meds. That was it. For today at least, he'd blame his unruly imagination on the meds.

"And don't scratch," she shouted to him from halfway down the hall.

Another quick perusal of the tabletop and he spotted a ballpoint pen. The kind with the pull off cap. It wouldn't reach all the way to his wrist, but the straight part might offer at least some relief. Twisting and turning his arm every which way possible, he failed miserably at finding any relief.

The slapping sound of bare feet against the old wooden floors grew closer before coming to a stop. "What are you doing?"

"Nothing." He dropped the pen cap onto the sofa.

"Right. Nothing." In loose fit sweats and a t-shirt, she headed into the kitchen shaking her head. Opening drawer after drawer, then banging cabinet doors open and shut, she stood, hands on hips, surveying the kitchen from one short end to the other.

"What are you looking for?"

"Something easier and safer than a steak knife."

That made him smile. Since they'd barely finished breakfast, and Lucy had promised soup for lunch, he doubted the knife was for cooking.

"Got it." She snapped her fingers and spun around, opening the pantry door. For a few seconds, she disappeared into the small space. He could hear her rummaging before she came out holding a plastic case. "This should work."

"This?"

"Bamboo skewers."

Great. She'd already driven into him, almost tripped into his lap, and now she wanted to stab him. "I don't know."

"It's perfect. Narrow, flexible, and the nub end is rounded and won't do accidental damage."

"Hm." He wasn't sure about this one.

"Trust me." She hurried back and Cole held his breath waiting to see if she would trip and go flying.

To his relief—or was it disappointment—she didn't fall into his lap. Seated on the coffee table, she leaned forward. As soon as she pulled the cap off the canister an odd smell smacked him in the face.

"Is that… gum?"

"Spearmint, actually. Someone must have spilled some essential oil in the drawer they were stored in."

"Or in the canister," he mumbled. He felt like he'd transported to the interior of a chewing gum factory. A stick or two was fine, but the cloying scent of this much mint was a bit much.

"Beggars can't be choosers."

She had a point. The itch inside his cast was reaching torturous proportions

"Let me have your arm."

He must have hesitated a moment too long.

"I can't hurt you. The edge is perfectly round."

Hesitantly, he stretched the wrist forward. The second she slid the flexible shoot of wood into the crevice, scraping against his skin, he could have leaned over and kissed her. Not a good idea.

CHAPTER SEVEN

The mumbled sounds of conversation drifted through the thin walls. Poppy Nelson turned the corner of the small cabin that the fireman and her sister were staying in. She had just enough time left on her lunch hour to drop off the soup Lucy had made and make sure her sister really was okay. Poppy couldn't begin to imagine how she'd feel if she'd hit a pedestrian with her car. Just the thought made her heart do a back flip and her mouth go dry. A muffled groan slowed her steps. A second guttural sound drifted through the cabin walls and Poppy picked up speed, hurrying to the front door.

"Oh, that feels so good," a male voice practically moaned. "Faster. Oh yeah, now you've got it."

Her hand wrapped around the doorknob, Poppy snapped straight in place.

"Would you stop squirming," her sister muttered. "You're going to break something."

Break something?

"You're not doing it fast enough. Let me show you how."

There were several logical possibilities for the exchange inside, but only one thing came to mind and she had no intention of turning the knob and finding out for sure. Taking a quiet step back to avoid being heard, she chuckled quietly to herself for being so careful. Who the heck inside would be paying any attention to her making noise out here?

The loud rumble of male voices in the distance grew louder— and closer. Ralph and the General were coming down the hill from Ralph's house. *Oh no.* She didn't have any choice. Banging on the door, she closed her eyes, turned the knob and hollered, "Ready or not, the General's on his way."

At the same moment she shoved the door open, Lily's voice rang out, "Now you've done it. I'll have to find some tweezers."

Tweezers?

"Poppy?" Lily said. "What are you doing here? And why is your hand over your eyes?"

Spreading her fingers apart like a Vulcan hand signal, Poppy opened one eye. Brother, did she feel the fool.

Fully clothed, her sister stood with something thin and pointy in her hand staring at Poppy as though she had snakes growing out of her head.

No defense like a good offense. "I'll do you one better. What are you doing?"

"Scratching his itch."

Her gaze darted quickly from Lily to Cole and back.

Rolling her eyes, her sister blew out a sigh. "In his cast. His arm is itchy." Lily waved whatever was in her hand in his direction. "Mr. Stubborn here insisted on rubbing too hard and we broke the bamboo skewer. Now the bottom half of it is stuck in his cast and I need to get it out. Though I doubt there's any extra long pair of tweezers here."

The rumble of laughter floated into the room seconds before the General. "Ralph and I are heading into town for an afternoon game of checkers at Floyd's. Thought we'd pop in a second make sure everything is going all right. You don't need anything?"

"I don't suppose you have a pair of tweezers in your pocket?" Sarcasm clearly laced her words.

The General squinted with confusion and then chuckled. "Nope. Can't say that I do."

Ralph shuffled around his friend moving closer to Cole, and nodded at him. "I'm Ralph. I live on the other side of the creek. You need anything this little lady can't do for you, just call on me."

"Thanks. Appreciate the offer." Cole smiled up at the older man.

Lily reached out and laid a hand on the old neighbor's arm. "I really am sorry for letting my car roll into your shed."

"Nothing to be sorry for." Eyes twinkling, Ralph smiled and turned to the General. "Ready?"

"All right then." Their grandfather clicked his heels and did a 180 degree perfect turn. "We'd better get going before Floyd thinks we skipped out on him."

"If you'll excuse me a minute, I'm going to see if by any miracle we have some tweezers in the bathroom." Lily scurried down the hall.

"I suppose I should introduce myself more formally. I'm Poppy, Lily's youngest sister."

"Nice to meet you. I'm Cole McIntyre."

He had a nice smile, the kind to put a person quickly at ease. For a few seconds she considered apologizing for the way she'd burst into the cabin, but as her great granny used to say, *"Better to keep your mouth closed and appear a fool than to open it and remove all doubt."*

Unexpectedly, his smile slipped and a crease formed between his brows. "Lily, Violet, Hyacinth, and now Poppy. You all have flower names?"

"That's right." Poppy smiled, pleased his frown hadn't come from something more serious. "We are the product of three wanna-be hippie sisters who named all of their daughters after flowers."

"Wanna-be?"

"Too young to actually be hippies, but old enough to remember, they grew up to be prominent citizens. Heavens, my Aunt Rebecca is about as prominent as they get, but they never gave up on the flower names."

"I see." The look on his face said anything but.

Rather than explain the family dynamics further, she showed him the container in her hand. "Lucy's soup. I popped in for lunch and am off to the church, but thought I'd save Lucy the delivery trip."

"Church." Cole glanced up at the clock. "Mass or a funeral?"

"Neither," Poppy chuckled. "I'm a bookkeeper at St Mary's. Funerals are Mom's department. Ever since my dad died she runs Lawford Funeral Home in town."

"Sorry for your loss."

"Thanks, but that was a long time ago."

"How about that." Lily trotted into the living room, triumphantly holding a pair of tweezers in the air.

"If you'll excuse me," Poppy said to Cole, "I'll go ahead and put this in the kitchen. Lucy sent enough for lunch and said if you two want more just let her know and she'll send another batch down."

"Thanks." Her brows curled in concentration, Lily sat beside her patient.

Poppy headed straight for the door. "I'll let myself out." It seemed only right since she'd let herself in.

"Thanks for the lunch." Cole grinned up at her. "Safe travels."

"I got it!" Grinning with satisfaction, Lily sprang up from the seat, the broken skewer in her left hand. "And thanks for saving me the trip to the house. If I left this guy alone," she waved over her shoulder at Cole, "who knows what else he'd break off trying to scratch the itch."

Poppy nodded at her sister, and with one hand on the door, considered the man on the sofa. Their mother was right. Sometimes fate showed a curious sense of humor.

• • • •

Bored with his book, Cole was pleased for an excuse to snap it shut. Today had been one heck of a day. Unexpected from dawn to dusk. Now, smiling at him, Lily approached with a dinner tray.

Not an ugly one in the bunch was the first thought that came to mind. Cole had met Violet, Cindy, and now Poppy. Though no one would say that sizing up a woman in a few minutes was his strong suit—just ask anyone about his ex—he was still pretty sure they were all nice people. The same way he was sure Lily's honest and caring nature was a rarity among modern day women living behind well-crafted facades.

As if it wasn't enough that she'd been serving him meals all day, the meat on his plate was cut up into small bite-size pieces. Though he felt like a toddler needing his mother to cut his food, not until he'd seen her handiwork had it dawned on him that for the next few weeks he would have to be a one-handed eater. "Where did you come up with frying steak like a chicken?" The last thing he needed while he was unable to exercise and burn calories was to be on a steady diet of fried foods and gluten heavy breads. His body must think he'd lost his mind. And yet, her eagerness to cook for him was…endearing.

Lily lifted a forkful of gravy-smothered mashed potatoes. "Afraid I can't take the credit for chicken fried steak. I first tried it during a trip to Houston for a cooking contest. Thought I'd died and gone to heaven. I have tweaked the white gravy recipe a bit, but not enough to lay claim to the concept."

He didn't know about the heaven part, but she was on the right track with died. He could almost feel his arteries clogging just looking at the dish. It had been years since he'd eaten ordinary white potatoes, and he didn't think he'd ever had anything even close to the white gravy smothered all over everything. Even the asparagus was smothered in the creamy sauce. Slowly sliding the first mouthful from his fork, he had to admit it wasn't half bad. By the second bite it was pretty good and by the third bite he decided he might be in trouble.

Under normal circumstances he would never have indulged in a meal like this. Though most of his buddies would work off the pizza calories and beer belly carbs, he'd learned from a college girlfriend that eating green and lean made a man feel better. His career demanded he stay in better shape than the average male his age and the right diet and daily workouts guaranteed that. Of course, with the injuries to his arm, shoulder and ankle, hitting the gym wasn't going be an option any time soon. Eating like this was definitely going to be a problem. Especially if everything she cooked tasted this good. He seriously needed to get out of here and go home. All he needed was to get through the night and tomorrow he'd figure out some excuse for heading back to his apartment.

"I've made a treat for tonight. Spitzbuben."

"Spit Who?"

Lily chuckled from deep down inside her, a rumbling that made him want to laugh too. "*Spiitzzzbuuben,*" she enunciated carefully.

"Sounds like a disease."

"They're German Christmas cookies."

"It's not Christmas."

"No, but they're my family's favorite. I don't make them often but I thought…" Her words trailed off.

She thought she could make things better with cookies? He'd watched her working away in the kitchen the better part of the afternoon. Diligently pounding at dough, rolling it out flat and starting again all over. The entire time, intent on her job and yet he was acutely aware of her keeping one eye on him. No doubt the cookies were loaded with butter and sugar and all things bad for the human condition.

A dirty dish in each hand, Lily carried them to the kitchen and came back to the sofa with a small plate stocked with tiny quarter-size cookies. Two coin-sized patties with jam-like filling in between. As if there wasn't going to be enough sweeteners already to send his blood sugar soaring and his pancreas into insulin overload, the treats were covered in powdered sugar.

At this point, with all the carbs and fats he'd consumed, one little cookie wasn't going to kill him. Picking one up carefully between two fingers, almost as if having more skin to cookie contact would increase the venomous qualities, he quickly popped the single bite-size confection into his mouth.

In seconds the plastic smile designed to hide his propensity to avoid sweets slipped. Tiny taste buds in every corner of his mouth did handsprings and back flips. These suckers were beyond amazing. It was all he could do to stop from moaning out loud. Had he ever had a cookie even close to this delicious? Beyond a doubt, this sucker was the cookie of all cookies. And he desperately wanted another.

Looking up at the tentative sweet smile waiting for his approval, his stomach did a back flip of its own. If given half the chance, this woman could be as lethal as her Spits-who cookies.

• • • •

Years ago, Katie O'Leary had shared her grandmother's secret cookie recipe with Lily. Not that Lily ever understood why a woman as Irish as the shamrock had a secret recipe for German cookies, but it didn't matter. She'd been honored that Katie had shared it with her. She'd also never had anyone not like the holiday treats. Except maybe one. With every small crunch of his teeth, she waited for the tell-tale moan, smile, popping eyes. Something that told her how delighted the consumer was. Not Cole. His face remained free of all emotions. Rather than having his smile broaden as she'd expected, it fell completely by the wayside. Had she been too distracted keeping an eye on him? Over or under added an ingredient? Or, heaven forbid, the wrong ingredient all together?

Her gaze shifted to the kitchen counters. This wasn't her kitchen. Even so, surely she couldn't have done anything as stupid as confusing salt and sugar. She turned her attention back to the man now swallowing slowly. When he seemed less than thrilled with dinner she thought for sure he'd love dessert. Yet he didn't look any happier now.

"That," he blew out a breath, "was delicious."

Not till a smile as wide as the lake appeared on his face did she believe him. "Have another."

"No." He shook his head and leaned back. "One is over my limit. Thank you."

"Oh." One? She withdrew the dish and just to make sure, picked one up with her free hand to taste for herself. The moment her lips sealed shut, the sweet flavors danced in her mouth. They were perfect. Just as they should be. Something had to be wrong with that man.

"Hello." Without knocking, her grandfather waltzed into the room. Clearly he intended to personally enforce the no fraternizing rule. Her grandmother, Ralph, and several more of the town busybodies followed behind him.

"So, you're Lily's firefighter." The predatory grin on Nadine Baker's face—ring leader for the unofficial Merry Widows Club—almost made Lily laugh. The startled spark in Cole's eyes definitely pushed a burst of giggles from her.

"Yes." The General nodded, pointing to a narrow space along the window without any furniture in the way. "Let's set the tables up over there."

"Tables?" Lily's gaze fell to the folded card table at his side and the one beside Ralph.

"We know Cole here shouldn't be trucking up to the house so we brought the house to him. Well, at least the tables and the company." Already on his way to the window, the General slid around Lily, not waiting for a response.

Unable to read the thoughts bouncing around behind Cole's steel gray eyes, she considered what an emotional rollercoaster today had been and testosterone heavy man or not, he had to be just as exhausted. Even if not emotionally, at least physically. "Can we have a rain check?

"Rain check?" The General stopped midstride. "Why?"

"Dear." Her grandmother sidled up beside him, her hand on her husband's shoulder. "It has been a very long day. Perhaps you can help our guest get ready for bed and let him get a good night's sleep."

"Oh, of course." Her grandfather beamed down at his wife with a devotion that words failed to describe. Had anyone else in the room said the same thing the General would have blustered and pushed his will on everyone. Not so with the woman he'd adored for almost all of his adult life. "Very good idea, dear." Spinning about, his attention landed on Cole. "Let's get you started."

"That won't be necessary, sir." Cole pointed to the scooter parked at the foot of the sofa. "I can get around well enough with that."

A deep furrow between his brows, the General studied the contraption then turned his gaze on Cole's injuries. The frown remained intent. Lily could see the thoughts spinning in his mind. She imagined he was calculating the repercussions of walking out that door and leaving Cole with only her for any assistance. She knew the moment he'd made up his mind. A brief nod dipped his chin against his neck. "I'm sure in your condition you'll sleep like a log tonight. We will see you in the morning."

"Wouldn't that be nice," Nadine practically purred.

Once again, the wide-eyed surprise on Cole's face had Lily covering her mouth with her hand to hide her amusement. She didn't know what was more entertaining, seeing the cougar side of Nadine, a woman almost old enough to be her grandmother, or the flash of shock on Cole's face.

"Tomorrow morning, sir," Cole responded naturally. Chain of command in the fire department and chain of command in the military had to be much the same.

"Very well." Grams placed a light kiss on her cheek and added a gentle reassuring pat on the arm before slipping away.

The crowd slowly ushered out. The door closed and locked behind them, once again it was Lily and Cole alone in the small cabin. In the dark of night. She thought back on the stubborn man, wincing in discomfort as he'd maneuvered himself into the bathroom earlier this afternoon. Stripping out of his jeans, one footed and one handed, might be more of a problem than she'd considered a few minutes ago. Maybe she'd been a little hasty hurrying her grandfather out the door.

CHAPTER EIGHT

The last traces of dinner cleaned up and put away, Lily sat in a comfy chair, pretending to read, and watching her guest, or patient, doze off on the sofa. She was glad he had a propensity for cat naps, which made her assigned task of not letting him sleep too long easier. The scooter had been the best suggestion Violet could have made. Lily couldn't begin to imagine how hard moving from room to room would have been for him. Or how much help she could have been.

His pills remained on the coffee table. He might be a precision freak, but she was pretty sure the bottles hadn't been touched all day. Shifting in place, his bad arm brushed against the sofa back, a low moan eased into more of a whimper behind a slow grimace.

Coming to her feet, she padded to his side and gently tapped his arm.

Immediately his eyes flew open and he sprang up, this time growling and grabbing the injured arm.

"Sorry, I didn't mean to startle you."

"You didn't. I've been conditioned to wake easily and fast. Usually jumping up first and asking questions later isn't so…challenging."

Lily reached behind her and grabbed a pill bottle. "These are for pain?"

"As needed."

"Have you taken one?"

"Don't need them."

She stared at him a moment, considering the best way to phrase this. Hardly knowing the man, she didn't have a clue how he'd react to her telling him what to do. "Perhaps it would help take the edge off that challenge."

"No." He swung his legs off the side, gingerly resting the bad foot on the floor. "Thank you, but no."

The peaceful lull of the last few hours had her forgetting about his stubborn side. "Very well." She returned them to the spot on the table. "It's getting late. Would you like a snack before bed?"

The way his eyes circled round, anyone would have thought she'd asked if he'd like a cyanide pill. "No, thank you. I'm still full from dinner."

"Well, I thought I would do some baking tonight to take over to the Inn."

"The Inn?"

Until this moment she hadn't realized they'd had almost no personal conversation. If the house wasn't full of people, or she wasn't in the kitchen cooking, then he was dozing on the sofa. "I bake for the Hilltop Inn. I was on my way to work this morning when… when…well."

A hint of a smile pulled to one side of his mouth. "That would explain the frock."

"Yes, I suppose it would." Usually she called it a jacket, but to some it might seem a frock.

"Do you always bake from here?"

"No. But under the circumstances, I'd rather not leave. I'll have to run over to Hart House for the ingredients, but I won't be long."

"Hart House? Not the grocery store?"

She shook her head. "No. Lucy will have everything I need and any store close enough to just pop over at this hour won't."

"I see." Pulling the scooter closer to him and lifting off the sofa, he leaned heavily on the contraption. He was definitely tired. "You don't have to change your routine for me. You can go home now. I'll be fine."

"Not the agreement."

"Agreement?"

"With the doctor. You were not coming home to be left alone." She inched forward. "Do you need some help?"

His head turned from side to side. "Nope. I can handle anything I need to do with my left hand.

"Okay." She nodded but watched very closely as he worked his way toward the bedroom.

Not wanting to look too conspicuous, she plopped herself down by the island. She'd been making a short list when the bedroom door inched open and Cole proceeded into the bathroom. So far, so good. Another few minutes passed and she wondered how long it takes a wounded man to get ready for bed. She didn't hear running water coming from down the hall, so what was taking him so darn long? She managed a few more notes and glances back and forth before the bathroom door eased open.

"I, uh, may have lied." The voice drifted down the hall before the door had been fully extended and she could see inside. "I think I need some help after all."

The sight of strong fireman Cole McIntyre twisted up in a t-shirt, his head half sticking out, the other half twisted in cotton had her quickly covering her mouth to hide her amusement. "Off or on?"

"On. Off was manageable. Though it makes no sense why on would be any worse, but for some reason it is."

She didn't believe for a minute it had been that easy. Stepping into the confined space, she eased the shirt off again. "Let's start over. It might be simpler that way."

"At this point, I'll try anything."

"We don't have to be that drastic." She could see the frustration taking over his face, the way his skin tensed under her touch. "Or maybe not." She chuckled.

"Not as easy as it looks?"

It would have been much easier if his arms weren't the size of a small baked ham. She maneuvered one way then the other, extremely careful not to jar the bad shoulder and giving it one good yank, the thing slipped away from his head. Holding the t-shirt in her hand, she looked down at the offending cloth. Definitely not as easy as it looked—in so many ways.

●●●●

"Okay." Eyes crossed and her cheeks puffed out just before her mouth twisted to one side, Lily blew at a loose strand of hair. She looked intent, focused, ridiculous, and incredibly likeable. At least Cole certainly thought so.

"First things first," she continued. "Do you by any chance have a button-down shirt?"

He shook his head. Who brings a button-down shirt for a week's stay at a rustic cabin by the water?

"Do you have anything bigger?"

"My workout shirts are double extra large."

Confusion clouded her gaze.

"I don't like to feel constrained when I'm doing a workout," he explained.

"Got it." That smile he was getting used to had returned. "Where do you keep it?"

He rolled back an inch or so to clear a path. "I'll get it."

Immediately, her hand shot out, grabbing his arm and stilling his plans. The touch was light, firm, ordinary and yet extra-ordinary. Her gaze locked with his and for a fraction of a moment, he simply couldn't have dragged his eyes away if the entire Marine Corps had insisted. How could the touch of a woman he knew not even twenty-four hours leave him so totally stunned?

"I, uh," she took a step back, "will get your shirt for you."

"Second drawer."

She nodded, backed out of the doorway and reappeared with an oversized t-shirt in hand.

"This should be easier. The neckline is even stretched."

"I can handle it this time." He wasn't all sure he wanted to risk having her near him again.

"Don't be silly." Blowing the same lock of hair that insisted on lying across her cheek, she rearranged the fabric, the sleeve taut between her hands. "Let's start with the bad arm. That's the one thing that cannot be twisted around in a wrestling match."

By the time he'd taken a few seconds to decipher exactly what she'd said, he found his bad arm carefully slipped into the sleeve of the shirt and gently nestled against him before she pulled the shirt over his head and then waited for him to slide his good arm into the other sleeve.

"And there you go." A smile bloomed as wide and satisfied as when Payton had proposed after tasting her baking.

"Thanks." From where he stood, the hall back to the living room looked a mile long and then some. As much as he hated to admit it, he was wiped out. The best thing for him would be a good night sleep. Tomorrow he'd be feeling more like his old self.

At least, that was his story and he was sticking to it. He hoped.

● ● ● ●

Lily waited until Cole was settled into his room and his eyes had fallen shut to run over to the main house. Nearing Hart House along the path, she could hear laughter coming from inside. The porch or enclosed veranda, depending on weather, had been the true heart of her grandparents' home. Friends, neighbors and guests could always leave their cares behind for a few hours, either seated at the card tables or swaying on the ancient, well-loved rockers.

Tonight she was too tired to even pass through the group for casual chit chat. Not to mention there was no such thing as quick on a card night. Common courtesy would have her visiting for a good long while and she didn't want to leave Cole alone for long, even if he did seem to be resting peacefully. Instead of facing the friendly gauntlet, she slid into the house from the kitchen door off the rear porch. In only a few minutes she'd bagged all the ingredients she needed and was on her way back to the cabin.

Veering right down the front hall, she peeked inside Cole's room. Pillows propped under his ankle, flat on his back, he was still sound asleep. Good, he needed his rest. So did she.

Tomorrow's cinnamon cranberry bread for the Inn wouldn't be her usual spread of baked choices, but at least the guests wouldn't be disappointed with only ordinary bread or English muffins. The Inn counted on her for unique breakfast treats and she didn't want to disappoint.

Making room on the small counter space, she was reminded why she didn't bake from home. Her mind also wandered to the storefront on Main Street. She'd kill for a chance to walk though it and get a better idea of the space. For years she'd had a general picture of how she wanted her kitchen laid out in her own bakery. If she had more money saved. If she could come up with one extra-ordinary item. If this had only happened in another year or two... If, if, if. What was it her grandmother always said, *if I had wheels I'd be a car.*

Mid-knead, a soft sound seemed to come from down the hall. She stilled, listening. Nothing more. Maybe it was the wind, or a prowling cat, or, heaven help her, a mouse. Though mice didn't moan. Neither did cats. Wiping her hands on a nearby kitchen towel, she padded down the hall, inched the door open and peeked in.

Cole had rolled to his side. His face pinched, his bad arm hung low and the pillows were less under him and more beside him. This wasn't going to work. What was called for was a sturdier cushion. Like from the sofa. What she had to figure out was how to get them under his ankle without waking him.

Trotting off to the living room, she grabbed a few cushions and hurried back to his room. The pain must have been too much even in his sleep. He'd turned over again onto his back and his face looked more relaxed. Careful to be quiet, she stood at the foot of the bed and considered her problem, afraid to actually lift his ankle with her hand for fear she'd hurt him or wake him up. The last thing she needed now was to explain why she was manhandling him in his sleep.

The best option meant lifting the top pillow his foot rested on, and quickly pull the other two pillows out from under him, and toss them to the floor. Forcing her lungs to release air, she paused a moment, noticing he didn't seem to feel her presence, and proceeded to glide the larger cushion underneath. The size and heavy fabric against the sheet would be less likely to slip around than the pillows.

Gently, she lowered his foot and waited for any response. Nothing. He didn't budge, didn't moan, didn't wake up. Mission accomplished. Had he been awake it would have been a fifteen minute battle over letting her help. The man was awfully stubborn. But she had to admit he was pretty nice too. Not that he'd done any grand gestures or anything, nor could he in his condition, but he'd yet to grumble or complain or point out that she was the reason he was in pain and uncomfortable. He'd not brought it up at all and *that* made him a nice guy in her book. Too bad she hadn't met him the way normal people do. She was pretty sure she'd like having Cole McIntyre as a friend.

CHAPTER NINE

Absolutely nothing about this morning had gone the way Lily expected. First, her plans of slipping out the door while Cole remained sleeping to deliver the breads flew by the wayside as soon as he crawled out of bed only minutes after she did. Why she'd thought he would sleep in, she didn't know. It was only reasonable. She had, after all, hit the man jogging at this forsaken hour of the morning only twenty-four hours ago.

The way she'd looked at it, she had two choices: call Barb to ask her to pop by and pick up the ready to bake pans, or wake one of her sisters to come and fireman-sit. Focused on the phone tightly gripped in one hand, a loud rapping against her kitchen window knocked the breath out of her. The unexpected face pressed against the glass had her nearly jumping out of her shoes. Good thing she didn't have anything breakable in her hands or it might have gone flying across the room.

To rise and shine before the sun was a habit her grandfather had no intention of breaking. Her grandma might be able to take the General out of the Marine Corps, but there was no taking the Marine Corps out of the General. At least she had someone to watch over Cole while she ran to the Inn.

The good thing about leaving a former Marine General in charge was that Cole didn't dare argue. Holding her breath and hurrying as quickly as she could without hitting anyone else on the road to work, she did her best to slip in and out of the kitchen at the Inn, but what was it they said about the best laid plans of mice and men?

"There you are." Barb Miller came running in from the front hall, tying an apron behind her back. "Margo's daughter has a slight fever so it's just us this morning."

Just us? Lily's gaze darted to the clock over the doorway.

"Oh good." Barb scanned the two trays Lily had brought. "Everyone loves your breads."

"I brought a strudel too. For the guests with more of a sweet tooth."

Having worked together for a few years now, Barb didn't need to wait for instructions, she was already sorting the pans and setting oven temps and timers. "How is your young fireman doing?"

"He's not mine."

"Of course he isn't." Over her shoulder, Barb shot Lily a grin that did nothing to add to the veracity of her agreement.

"I'll help get these started while you set the table, but I won't be able to stay through breakfast."

Famous last words. The Inn was full and there was no way Barb could handle the baking and the cooking and the inn keeping on her own. Long after she'd intended, Lily finally made it back to the lake, and rushing down the cobbled path, she almost went flying face first across a tray of begonias waiting to be planted. Who the heck left them sitting there? Had the small flowers been here all night?

Brushing herself off, she hurried into the cabin. Not that she feared any harm would come to Cole under her grandfather's watchful eye, she just wasn't so sure what the man might say to him, especially about there being easier ways for Lily to catch a man than mowing him down.

Her grandfather's deep voice carried across the small space. The words *stones*, *copycat* and *not anymore* told her the retired general was explaining about the building of the point. How after one of the neighbors tried to outdo the manmade land extension one of her greats had built by hand, the lake planning commission had changed the rules to prohibit more land masses from jetting out into the beautiful waterway.

"Oh, you're back." Her grandmother's voice grabbed Lily's attention away from the older man seated across from her guest and drew it to the injured fireman.

His arms up like a referee's goal hand signal, Cole sat catawampus, one foot on the floor, and one foot elevated on the sofa, helping Grams ball up her yarn. He looked ridiculous, seriously intent, and absolutely adorable.

"Sorry I'm late," Lily muttered.

"We're just about finished here." Her grandmother smiled up at

Lily and turned to her husband. "I think I'd like to add another shade or two to the pattern. Would you be able to give me a lift?"

Unlike most times when her grandfather would respond quickly in the affirmative of whatever his wife had asked him, this time the General frowned slightly, shifting his gaze from Lily to Cole and back to his wife. "Nora's?"

"Yes, dear." Fiona Hart wound the last strand around the massive ball, leaving Cole's hands free once again.

The General cast his glance back and forth, the furrow between his brows set deep, his lips pressed tightly. For the first time that she could remember, Lily felt sure her grandfather was going to deny Grams her request in order to remain as chaperone.

On a resigned sigh, the General eased the crease between his bushy brows and nodded. "I'm ready when you are."

It only took her grandmother another couple of minutes to gather her latest project, whatever it might be, into her bag and stand up, ready to move on.

"If you need anything," the General spoke to Cole, "anything at all, make sure to call the main house. Lucy will gladly come running."

Lily nodded. "I will." The family housekeeper and cook had been around since before she or any of her cousins were born. Lily didn't doubt that Lucy would entertain a viper for the good of the family. Of course, she'd probably sing an entire chorus from *Hello Dolly* first, but by gosh she'd be there for everyone.

At the front door, the General cast his gaze around the room one more time. "Remember—"

"If you're not home yet, call the house for help. Got it. Really, I do."

"Harold," Grams called from up the walkway.

The General nodded at Lily and pulled the door shut behind him.

"You don't think he's still stuck on that fraternization thing, do you?" Cole asked, studying the front door intently.

"I honestly haven't the slightest idea." She actually didn't have a clue to a lot of things at the moment. From the incapacitated fireman in her charge, to the missing signature item for her dream job, to the General's odd behavior, Lily decided there was only one solution. Bake.

• • • •

The more Cole tried to figure out what was going on around him, the more he decided Alice in Wonderland had nothing on him. He might as well have fallen down a rabbit hole.

"Well." Lily slapped her hands together and rubbed vigorously. "Hungry?"

Cole shook his head. "Your grandfather made us all eggs and bacon."

Eyes wide with surprise, Lily paused mid-step and gaped at him. "My grandfather?"

"Yes. He, uh, seemed to know his way around the kitchen."

"My grandfather? General Hart?" she repeated.

"Does he not cook often?"

"Often?" Lily tipped her head and continued on path to the kitchen. "I don't remember ever seeing him cook in my entire life. At least not anything more than marshmallows over the fire."

Right now, if he had two good feet, Cole would have been on them and following Lily into the kitchen. Little more than a day of rest and he'd had enough.

"Looks like my grandfather has many hidden talents." She lifted a paper towel off the dish of leftover bacon. "He cleans up pretty well too."

"I imagine he wasn't always a general."

Lily laughed. "No, I suppose not, but I doubt he's had to clean a kitchen since his days at Annapolis."

He doubted the old guy would have had kitchen duty there either. Tired of lying on the sofa, Cole spun around, setting his feet on the ground.

"And where do you think you're going?" Lily pinned him with a narrowed gaze.

He didn't know, but he was sure there was only one answer that she couldn't object to. "The bathroom. Is that okay?"

"Oh, of course." She maneuvered around the tiny island. "I'll help."

"Really?" He bit back a smile. It wasn't easy. The way her

cheeks flushed a pretty shade of pink tugged at the smile center in his brain.

"I mean, uh, you know, getting there."

"I'll be fine."

It took her a moment to nod and turn back to the refrigerator. Now that he'd committed, he made a quiet show of easily standing and riding the scooter to the bathroom and then back again. "So what do people do for entertainment around here?"

That pretty splash of pink filled her cheeks again. "Lots of things."

"Such as? Because it's not watch TV. I thought everyone in the world had cable or satellite."

"The whole idea is to come out here to relax, unplug, and learn to enjoy your friends and family, or whoever you've come out to be with. Unless you have one particular cell phone service, Mother Nature is a great help at forcing people to cut their ties to the outside world. Usually almost every night when the weather is nice, there's a group of people playing cards on my grandfather's porch."

Cole eased onto the sofa, keeping one eye on the kitchen to see if Lily was going to supervise. Much to his surprise, she didn't come running over to make sure his foot was elevated high enough. "That would be the card tables and people who arrived last night. What do they play?"

Lily opened and closed a cabinet, then another. "Mostly whist, but they've been known to play a hand or two of poker. Sometimes in the afternoons Grams will get a canasta game going, but mostly she just likes to tinker with her projects."

"Yes, she showed me before volunteering me to help with the yarn." It would be interesting to see how the project turned out. According to Mrs. Hart, after she had enough squares made they would get attached and turned into a blanket. Apparently her last attempt at knitting didn't fare so well. Something about dropped stitches. Based on the few mismatched sized samples she'd shown him, he wasn't all that sure that this attempt at crochet was going to be any better. But he had to admit he had fun listening to the old lady prattle on about her granddaughters and how proud she was of them. Her Lily of course getting the most airtime.

"That was very nice of you," she said while her head was in the fridge.

Cole shrugged. "It's not like I had anything else to do. Besides, she's a nice lady."

She slammed the fridge door shut, and hands on her hip, walked to the small pantry. "I hope my grandfather didn't talk your ear off."

"Actually, it was your grandmother who did most of the talking while the General cooked. He didn't join the conversation until after he'd finished cleaning up the kitchen."

Opening and closing the pantry door with barely a glance inside, Lily sighed.

"What are you looking for?"

"Nothing in particular. Just doing an assessment. I definitely need to hit the grocery store. I don't even have enough things here to make you a decent lunch."

"Oh, Lucy dropped off a casserole. It should be in the fridge."

"Yeah, but there are no sides." She seemed hesitant to leave the kitchen. He had a feeling this was her domain. Where she was the most comfortable.

Actually, he'd rather skip the casserole and make a nice kitchen sink salad, but he had a feeling the folks around here would have a heart attack at that suggestion. "So," he glanced around the room, almost expecting to see something different than he'd seen every other time he'd looked around in the last day, "besides playing cards, what else do people do here?"

"In the warmer weather there's hiking, waterskiing, swimming, horseshoes, bocce, barbecues, bonfires…"

"All outdoor activities. What do they do inside?" Heading off that sweet blush, he quickly added, "There has to be something else a family can do besides play cards."

She nodded. "Every cabin should be stocked with board games and puzzles."

"Puzzles? That could be fun. Where are they kept?"

A broad smile on her face, she nodded and crossed the room to a cabinet by the window. "What do you like? Landscapes, florals, cars, planes…"

The cabinet doors open, he could see ceiling to floor shelves crowded with puzzle boxes, games. And not just board games, he was pretty sure he could see pickup sticks, bingo, and a few other things he couldn't quite make out from this distance. Definitely plenty to keep a family from boredom on a string of rainy days. "I don't suppose they have a fire truck?"

"Actually," she stretched up on her tippy toes took hold of the box and turned around smiling at him, "we do. Dalmatian and all." It only took a minute for Lily to clear the coffee table, sit closer to him, and spread out the pieces. "I like to start with the edges. You?"

"Works for me." Together they sifted through the thousand pieces of cardboard, the pile of straight edges growing to one side.

One by one Lily had hunted down three of the corners. Lips pressed tightly together, the tip of her tongue peeking out at one end of her mouth, she looked totally adorable searching for that last anchor piece. So enthralled with watching her eyes sparkle as she sorted and separated, he'd forgotten his assigned task of locating all the blue sky pieces for the top of the puzzle.

"Got it!" Bubbling with delight, Lily held up the fourth corner piece, showing it off with as much pride as a kid with a new toy at Christmas. The old cliché *a breath of fresh air* made so much sense. Who knew with the right company, even a silly jigsaw puzzle could be fun. Maybe going back to his empty apartment after tomorrow wasn't such a great plan after all?

CHAPTER TEN

"Next time we pick a puzzle with more colors." Lily turned the red piece in all directions as she searched for a match. Despite grumbling about the lack of diversity in the puzzle, she was having a much nicer time than she'd expected.

"Try this one." Cole handed her a piece. "It has a darker nub. Might work better on your side."

The guy had an eye for detail. Despite the sky being all blue, he'd managed to put most of the upper half together faster than she'd done one little corner of landscaping rocks and firehouse bricks.

"Bingo!" Snapping it into place, she bounced in her seat singing 'Another One Bites the Dust.'

Shaking his head, Cole laughed. "Heaven knows how you'd react if you ever won the lottery."

Lifting her gaze to the ceiling, she closed one eye and then nodding, looked back at him. "That would have to be 'Celebration'." Both hands up in the air, palms out, she put a little shoulder action into the popular Kool and the Gang tune.

"Ah." Cole chuckled and snapped another puzzle piece into place. "So the quiet granddaughter has another side."

"Not everything is as it appears." Not looking up, she rummaged through the pieces for something with a little hint of a yellow flower petal and continued humming the upbeat tune. "Nothing is ever black or white. Life is full of grays."

"But I suspect your life has a lot more pinks and purples and bright colors then you let on."

"Not really."

"No? Why don't I believe you? What's your favorite memory from growing up here?"

"Summer."

"More specific, please."

She straightened and stared out the large picture window. So many happy memories with her family and cousins. Every child should grow up playing in the woods, on the sand, in the water. "Bonfires. I especially loved being out by the water at night, the stars shining bright, and cooking s'mores over the open fire."

"So everything really does come back to food for you?"

Lily laughed. She hadn't really looked at it that way, but maybe he was right. "I also liked playing tricks on the football team but that's a story for another time."

"The football team?"

"There's something about sports and testosterone that turns ordinary little boys into arrogant teens. Everyone once in a while it was good to deflate their egos a bit."

"Oh, this I want to hear." Cole leaned back in his chair and crossed his arms. Looking her over from top to bottom, his actions were punctuated with the rumbling of his stomach.

Lost in the fun she was having with Cole and the puzzle, Lily hadn't kept track of time. "You must be starved. I'll heat up lunch."

"I want to hear about the football team's deflating."

"One time," she washed her hands at the sink, "a friend and I hid all their clothes while they were skinny dipping in the lake."

Cole's eyes popped open wide. "Okay, I wasn't expecting that much deflating."

"Let me guess." Lily kicked the fridge door shot with her foot and set the casserole on the counter. "You played football?"

"Guilty as charged."

"Quarterback?"

"Actually," his eyes reflected surprise, "yes."

It wasn't such a leap. He was strong and lean, with arms that could easily toss a football across the field. She'd have been more surprised if he'd told her he'd been the chubby nerd.

Removing the foil, she glanced at the dish. "Oh, this is one of my favorites."

"What is it?"

"Lucy's potato chip tuna casserole."

She glanced up just in time to see him wince before smiling. "Lucy seems like quite a character."

"You could say that." She grabbed a potholder in each hand.

"For as long as I can remember, Lucy's been a part of this family. I think she's the one who taught me my love of baking."

"So Lucy likes to bake too?"

"A little. She likes baking cookies, but nothing complicated. She swears any attempt at bread tastes more like a paper weight, and her soufflés make great doilies."

Cole chuckled. "Neither a good thing."

"Nope. But it turns out I love baking. I like cooking too. But I love baking." She slid the tuna noodle casserole into the oven and closed the door. Pulling the dish of spitzbubens from the counter, she walked back to where he was resting. "I know it's not good to have dessert first but just a few to tide you over won't hurt."

He eyed the dish warily. So much so, she actually looked down to make sure she grabbed the right plate and wasn't handing him something outlandish like eggshells for the compost pile.

"I promise I won't tell your mother," she teased, trying to break the oddly tense moment.

His gaze lifted from the plate to her. "Excuse me?"

"Everyone's mother drums it into us not to spoil our supper. I guess I was just trying to be funny."

"Oh. Sometimes I can be a bit dense. You know, leftover jock syndrome." He smiled, bringing a twinkle to his eyes, and picked up a cookie. "Normally I don't eat a lot of sweets. But these cookies are so good they could easily become addictive."

That made her want to grin like the Cheshire cat. "That's what everyone tells me. But a little sugar once in a while isn't all bad."

"But it's not once in a while. It's in everything. Processed foods are filled with sugar and preservatives and additives and the list goes on and on."

She plopped in the seat across from him and pointed to the kitchen. "Would that have anything to do with all those canisters on the counter?"

"It does."

"And all the salad fixings that Gabe brought?"

He nodded. "My job requires that I be in excellent shape. The equipment we carry alone requires me to stay beyond fit, never mind if we have a bad day and I have to carry somebody out, or more than one somebody. A body needs proper fuel, much the way a high-performance race car would."

"Carbs are fuel. Didn't anyone ever tell you that professional athletes often eat pasta before a big game?"

"Pasta is a complex carb. That isn't the same thing as fried foods or a bag of cookies."

"Noted." She'd take a bag of her cookies over his green gunk any day. "I'll make sure to put fresh meats and vegetables on the grocery list. Or are you vegetarian?" She held back a soft moan. "Oh, please don't tell me you're vegan. The world would be such a happier place if everybody used butter."

Cole snapped another piece into the puzzle. The soft rumble of his laughter made her want to smile. She liked the sound of it. "No, I'm not vegan. When I eat any meat, though, I do prefer grass-fed, organic, and hormone free."

"That I can do." She looked around at the last couple of the puzzle pieces on the table, wondering what she could bake that would be both fun and healthy.

"Looks like we have a problem." Cole pressed one piece, then the next into place and leveled his gaze with hers.

"I hate it when this happens." Lily leaned back in her chair. Nine hundred and ninety-nine pieces nicely fit together and one gaping hole.

"Maybe we should mark the top of the box for the next person."

"Or send it off to recycle and replace it."

"Or that." He smiled.

The oven timer sounded and Lily sprang from her seat. Who'd have thunk all those years ago when Lily was pranking the football team that one day she'd be confined to quarters with a quarterback? The whole idea made her want to giggle like a high school freshman. Lily and the quarterback.

• • • •

After the last puzzle he'd dozed off briefly and awoken to the sounds of Lily moving around in the kitchen. If she was making more of those cookies, he was in big trouble. At this rate, with all the high fats, high carb, and high sugar foods, Cole would have to double his workout regime sooner than later. Easing onto the scooter, he rolled across the small cabin. "What's cooking?"

"Brownies." Hands that could have belonged to a concert pianist turned the spatula, folding ingredients together in a bright red bowl. The dimple in her cheek belied the intensity of her gaze as the mixture thickened.

An empty can of pumpkin caught his eye. "Pumpkin?"

"I'm playing a little." She stuck her finger in the batter then into her mouth and shook her head.

"What exactly are you trying to do?" Cole shifted from the scooter to stool beside her.

"You got me thinking."

He nodded.

"I've always baked with real butter, real sugar, but maybe..." Her words trailed off as she took another taste.

"Have you tried apple sauce?"

"Of course." Snapping her fingers, her face lit up much the way it had done every time she'd snapped a puzzle piece in place.

So many things surprised him lately. How much he had enjoyed sitting still on the sofa working together on jigsaw puzzle. How his own cheeks tugged his face into a smile every time she squealed with glee over a simple matching piece. How his chest expanded like a proud peacock at bringing that twinkle to her eyes. And how much he would probably like standing beside her, chopping vegetables, bumping elbows, sharing smiles, really cooking together. The thoughts had him considering what it would be like to do other mundane daily routines. How much fun would she make changing the sheets, doing laundry, vacuuming, dusting? The list was endless, and with every passing moment, he found himself filling in the blanks and enjoying the scenes his mind created.

The squeaking from the front door hinges interrupted the picture in his mind.

"Yoo hoo," a female voice called, hurrying past them into the kitchen, her arms laden with brown grocery sacks. "There's more in the car."

Lily immediately sprang back, flinging her arms around the

guest before the lady had completely set the packages down. "Oh my gosh, Iris! What on earth are you doing here? Aren't you supposed to be in Thailand?"

"*Supposed to be* is the key phrase." The petite blonde returned the ardent embrace. "I'm just here for tomorrow and then I have to head back to the city. The Throckmortons are driving me crazy. If they think I'm climbing mountains in Tibet or freezing in Antarctica, they can find themselves another nanny."

"That bad?" Lily followed the young woman out the door, their voices drifting off.

Cole wasn't sure if the woman was a sister or a cousin. From what he remembered hearing from the General the day he'd done the inspections, there were nine granddaughters from three daughters. He remembered because the way the General had explained he had one daughter here, another in Boston and another in New York, the opening ditty from a later season of the old Charlie's Angels TV show about the angels coming from three different cities came to mind. The show had been one of his mom's favorites and he was pretty sure he'd seen every episode thanks to retro reruns.

The chatter from outside grew louder as the two women came into the house carrying more groceries. Not being able to hop up and help had his pleasant afternoon shifting into one of frustration and restlessness. So much for learning to enjoy being laid up for a while.

"There are days when I can't believe those two self-centered spoiled brats are the same adorable children I've lived with for the last three years. I mean, how does any human being change so dramatically so fast?"

"No clue, but the answer is probably the same for a few adults I know."

"Sorry I can't offer to lend a hand," Cole said, as if it weren't obvious why he couldn't help.

"Oh." Lily dropped the bag she carried quickly onto the island. "Iris, this is Cole, the man I, uh, am helping while he's laid up. Cole, this is my cousin Iris."

"Pleased to meet you," the woman said with a sudden air of polish he hadn't expected from someone who up until a few minutes ago had been chattering away like one of the teenagers she'd been complaining about.

"Sit down and tell me everything." Lily emptied a bag.

Iris shook her head. "Sorry, I still haven't reported in to the General. I came from the One Stop for some of Katie's soda bread and she asked if I could bring a few groceries to you here at the Willow guest cottage." Her gaze drifted casually to Cole and his leg resting on the scooter. "Looks like Katie didn't fill me in on everything."

"It's a long story. It started yesterday morning when he was jogging and I was heading to work—"

"Your cousin," he interrupted, "is being a good sport and taking care of me while I'm a bit," he extended his broken wrist without moving his shoulder, "incapacitated."

The way Iris looked at him then her cousin, he was sure she knew there was a lot more to the story than what he'd just shared. Maybe he shouldn't have stepped in, but the look of embarrassment in Lily's eyes as she began to explain to Iris why she was here made him want to spare her from reliving the story once again.

"I see." Iris nodded. "I'd love to stay and hear more, really I would," her eyes twinkled at her cousin, "but I need to get to the house before the General calls in the troops to look for me."

Lily reached for another grocery bag. "Join us for dinner?"

"You're not coming to the house?"

"Cole needs to elevate his leg for at least another day and then take it easy for a couple of weeks."

"I'm a big boy. I can stay home alone."

"And off your feet?" Lily actually rolled her eyes. A little more than a day and she already had his number.

"Except for the last few minutes, I've been good today, haven't I?"

Lily closed the fridge door. "Maybe, but still…"

"You've already turned your life upside down to help me, the least I can do is stay off my feet so you can have dinner with your family."

Iris quietly followed the conversation with the same interest as a spectator at the final round of Wimbledon.

"Besides," Lily stabbed at the meat she'd unwrapped, "I had

Katie send me over a couple of steaks and some fresh asparagus. You don't mind butter, right?"

"Butter's fine." In moderation, but now probably wasn't the time to mention it. He was almost flattered that after their brief conversation she'd taken steps to cook for his diet. He wasn't going to assume the baking efforts were on account of him as well.

"I thought we'd keep it simple. Lean New York strip with sautéed mushrooms and steamed asparagus. Will that work?"

"Yes, ma'am." Cole gave her a left-handed salute, pleased when the gesture brought a smile to her face.

"That sounds like my cue to leave." Iris gave her cousin another hug, spun on her heel, and got to the front door just as it squeaked open again.

"Iris!" Violet stood in the doorway, holding a folded card table. "I didn't know you were coming."

"Neither did I until this morning."

"Oh, this is going to be so fun. I want to hear all about your latest adventures."

Iris rolled her eyes and groaned softly.

"Okay," Violet picked up the table and waggled her brows, "not the response I was expecting."

"Long story." Iris shrugged. "I need to get to the house and let the General know I'm here."

"Oh, don't bother. He's on his way. He and Ralph have the folding chairs."

"Folding chairs?" Lily looked up from the kitchen.

Violet hefted one shoulder in a playful shrug. "Looks like you're hosting fun and games tonight."

The next thing Cole knew, the tiny cabin overflowed with people. In the kitchen, Lily's sisters, Cindy the veterinarian, Poppy the youngest, and Callie, short for Calytrix, laughed and giggled with their cousins Violet and Iris while the General explained to him the finer points of whist.

"All right, everyone." Lily came into the room holding a plate in each hand. "Dinner time."

First she served the General, then she set a plate in front of Cole. One by one the sisters and cousins came from the kitchen each carrying a plate. His mouth watered at the sight of the sizzling steak. Everyone settled in on the chairs, and the blessing said, Cole dug in.

It only took a few bites for him to realize something was wrong. Very wrong. It started with a scratchiness around his gums and down his throat. He took two long gulps of water and knew he needed to act. Not even thinking about his ankle, he pushed to his feet. Focusing wasn't coming easy.

"Whoa." Lily sprang up almost as fast as he had. "Where do you think you're going?"

He managed to mumble "Benadryl" when he noticed one of the cousins, or was it a sister, hurried to his side.

A female voice asked, "Do you have food allergies?"

He nodded, trying to shake the fog from his brain, suddenly fighting for a deep breath.

"I saw some Benadryl in the cupboard." Lily bolted over the ottoman and sprinted into the kitchen.

The next thing he knew, Lily held a pill and another glass of water for him to swallow. How could he possibly be reacting to steak and asparagus? He didn't know how or why, but he was absolutely positive he was in big trouble.

CHAPTER ELEVEN

Working with food most of her life, Lily recognized the beginnings of anaphylaxis from the strange way Cole had stared at his plate to the almost aimless way he'd stood. "What are you allergic to?"

"Pitted fruits," he mumbled, gasping for a deep breath. "Pen."

Cindy, who had been standing nearby from the moment he pushed off the sofa, waved a hand at him. "Do you have an epi pen?"

The way Cole moved his jaw, Lily had this horrible feeling his tongue might be swelling. Dear Lord, wasn't it enough she ran him down with her car, now she has to kill him with...what? There was no fruit in the dinner.

"My bag," he gasped.

Lily and her sisters bolted over the furniture and down the hall. She was the first to arrive, and grabbing his toiletry kit, practically shot out of the room waving the thing in her hand.

"I've called 911. Ambulance is on the way," the General announced.

Lily handed the pen off to her cousin the veterinarian. Lily might be great at injected turkeys, but she wasn't about to practice on this human.

Jabbing his thigh with the contraption, Cindy coaxed him into talking. "Are you allergic to anything else?"

"What?" he mumbled.

"Cole." Lily snapped her hand in front of him. "What else are you allergic to?"

He blinked twice. Despite his labored breath, he seemed to be breathing a tad easier. "Shrimp."

At least she was sure she hadn't given him fruit or shrimp.

"I'm going to see if you've been bitten by something. Okay?" Even though Cindy had asked permission she didn't wait for an answer before examining up and down his arms, between his fingers, and moving on to his neck.

Cole nodded, then sucked in another breath. "Sesame."

Sesame? She hardly ever cooked with sesame oil. Had someone before her contaminated the grill with sesame oil? Would it matter at this point?

"So far I don't see anything." Cindy examined his good leg and was unstrapping the boot on his injured ankle when it dawned on Lily to check the seasonings she'd used.

The jar was standard cooking stock in all the cabins. She'd poured on some Worcester sauce and then sprinkled the organic no salt seasoning. Onion, garlic, black pepper, she continued reading. Midway down the list of the ingredients there it was staring at her. Sesame. "It's the seasoning I used. It has sesame in it."

"How are you feeling?" Cindy asked.

Cole answered the question, but his gaze fell on Lily in the kitchen. "Better. Still hurts to breathe."

"The ambulance should be here any minute." The General kept an eye on his watch.

Lily hurried around the counter and came to a stop beside him. "I'm so sorry. I should've asked."

"Should we maybe try to get him ready somehow?" Poppy asked, her eyes round like a frightened owl. Lily's baby sister had always been the sensitive one in the family, taking everything to heart.

"Do you think you can balance on the scooter?" Cindy asked.

His chest heaving, Cole turned to look at Cindy but didn't say anything. The sound of the sirens in the distance broke the silent pause that had settled on the room, waiting for Cole to respond.

"I'll go up the drive and wave them down." Poppy jumped up and ran to the door.

Callie sprang to her feet. "I'll go with you."

Frozen in place, Lily clutched the stupid jar of seasoning as the sirens grew louder. The same two men who had taken care of Cole yesterday morning came rushing into the cabin.

"You again," Jason teased while swiftly getting Cole from the sofa to the gurney. "I see you're single-handedly trying to keep us in business."

Lily swallowed a moan. If anything, it was her fault, not his.

The EMT continued to ask Cole questions, but she didn't hear a word, her gaze landed on the cut kit at the ready in case Cole needed a tracheotomy. Her stomach rolled and pitched. What had she done this time?

"Let's boogie," the other EMT said, already rolling Cole out the door. "You coming with us?" He directed the question at Lily.

"Yes," she answered without hesitating.

"We'll follow in the car," someone said. She didn't even know who. She was already trotting after the two men and saying her prayers.

• • • •

Cole had the mother of all headaches and a pain in his thigh to match. So far, the ER team had taken his blood pressure, his heart rate, and measured his blood oxygen level with the pulse oximeter.

"Drink this." The nurse handed him another glass of water. "How long has it been since you used the EpiPen?"

Five minutes. Ten. Maybe twenty. Cole had no idea. "I don't know, but the General gave the exact time to Jason."

"Yes. According to the report it's been almost twenty minutes. Does that sound right?"

"Sure."

"Are you on any medications?"

Cole shook his head and then thought to answer instead. The doctors needed to know he was feeling better. More clear-headed. "No."

"Do you know how this happened?"

"Yes. I'm allergic to sesame products and the seasoning on the steaks had sesame in it."

"Good. Good. All right." The doctor took a step back. "I think the worst is behind you. I'm going to give you a prescription for prednisone."

"No, thank you."

"If you know to carry an EpiPen then you should know the drill. This will reset your system and add an extra layer of protection."

"I don't like taking steroids. I should be fine now."

The doctor lowered his chin and looked at Cole over the rim of his glasses. "Humor me. You could have died."

Suddenly Cole was very glad that Lily had stayed in the waiting room this time. Had she heard those words, he was pretty sure they would have made a difficult situation even worse. It didn't take a genius to know she already felt mortified at having sent him to the hospital yesterday. This evening's accident had to be eating at her. And he didn't like that.

"Your entourage is asking about you." One of the nurses popped her head inside. "And the pretty redhead who rode here in the ambulance with you is also wearing a rut in the floor. Shall I have her come in?"

While Cole had gotten the same doctor who had treated him yesterday, this was a different nurse. He nodded then almost laughed. Less than two days ago the last person he wanted in the waiting room, never mind here in the ER with him, had been Lily Nelson. Today things didn't seem right without her.

The nurse turned in place and walked briskly toward the waiting room doors.

"I don't think we need to admit you," the doctor continued. "But I do want to keep you here for a couple more hours of observation. Then I'll tell your lady friend what to look for tonight."

"I'll be fine." Cole was breathing so much easier, he was ready to go home now.

"Seems I've heard that song before." Lily came through the curtain wall, a tense smile failing to mask how truly shaken the events of the afternoon had left her.

"The lady is right. You're going to lay back and relax and I'll let you know when you'll be released." Letting his scolding scowl slip away, the doctor faced her. "If he's going to keep getting into trouble like this, you may want to consider locking him in the closet for a few years, or decades."

Lily nodded at the doctor and sucking in a long deep breath, inched closer to Cole's bed. Once again plastering on a brave smile. "Considering I've almost killed you—twice—my closet may not be the best place to keep you safe."

From the other side of the closed dividing curtain, the doctor's footsteps could be heard with his low voice muttering, "Third time better not be a charm."

"See!" Bright green eyes glistened with building tears.

"Hey, he was only joking." Cole resisted the urge to reach out and brush away the tears.

Her lids batted furiously up and down in a vain effort to stem the impending flow. "That doesn't change anything. It's like I'm a jinx around you."

"There's no such thing as a jinx."

"I know that. Or at least I used to, but I've never almost killed someone twice in two days."

"Lily." He stuck his good hand out, silently urging her closer. It took three minced steps before her hand was within snatching distance. "Life has no guarantees. Shit happens. If I'd been grilling a steak, I might very well have used the seasoning—"

"You would have read the label."

"No. Not for a salt substitute. I honestly only read labels on seasonings for Asian recipes. Not steak." He wasn't going to mention that he rarely used premixed ingredients and stuck to mostly organic whole foods. "Besides having taught me to read all labels from now on no matter what, I could make a case for you've actually saved my life."

"Hardly."

"If I'd been the one cooking and used that seasoning, I would have been alone and unable to get to medication."

"Cindy gave you the epinephrine."

"You noticed something was wrong. Without the Benadryl, I might not have been lucid enough to tell you my allergies. And had I been alone I'd have never gotten to the EpiPen." He squeezed her hand, pleased she hadn't made an effort to pull away. "I am grateful you were there for me."

Her eyes blinked a few times before a weak smile tipped the corners of her mouth. "For a former jock, you're not so bad."

Not exactly the reaction he'd been expecting, but he'd accept whatever positive thoughts he could get at the moment. "Not so bad?" he teased.

Her smile grew a little brighter. "Not bad at all?"

The twinkle slowly replacing the tears eased an unexpected pressure on his chest that had nothing to do with his allergies. He wasn't quite sure what to make of it, but he did know one thing—he'd have to work on changing not-bad-at-all to totally-freaking-awesome. And he had less than a week to do it.

• • • •

"There you are." The General stopped mid-stride at the site of Lily's approach. Her entire family currently at the lake had gathered in the waiting room for moral support. Her mom sat close to her youngest daughter, offering silent comfort. Normally it would take an act of God to keep her mom, the funeral director, from leaving her post if there was a scheduled wake, like tonight. Apparently a daughter's near miss at manslaughter rated right up there. Violet had taken up her spot on the floor, sitting cross-legged and eyes closed. Even her cousin Iris sat with Callie and Cindy chatting. Installed in a comfy easy chair, her grandmother worked diligently on her latest effort at a crochet masterpiece, but it was her grandfather whose ever constant show of family strength made nervous pacing look more like a military parade. "What's the prognosis?" he asked.

"All in all, we dodged a bullet. They are keeping him a little longer for observation. But he'll be able to come home after that."

"If you ask me," their neighbor Ralph, who had insisted on coming with everyone for moral support, put down the magazine he'd pretended to read and flashed a cocky grin, "seems like an awful lot of trouble on the young man's part to avoid your grandfather and me mopping the floor with him at whist."

Lily tried really hard to smile at the old man's attempt to lighten the mood. "Somehow I don't think that's what happened here."

By now, Violet had pushed to her feet, and stood beside her cousins. "So what's the game plan now?"

"I have to keep a lookout for any signs of recurring difficulties for the rest of the night." She didn't even want to consider how differently things could have turned out this evening.

Violet nodded, her eyes twinkling. "I'm in."

"Me too." Callie slipped her hand around Lily's waist and

squeezed.

Her mother came up on her other side and kissed her cheek. "What do you need us to do?"

"Nothing really." Working with foods for as long as she had, Lily had seen more than her share of allergic reactions at all stages. She understood exactly what to keep an eye out for and what the risks were long before the doctor intercepted her on the way to the waiting room with his list of cautions.

"Well," Virginia Hart Nelson tucked a stray shock of hair behind her daughter's ear, "there may be nothing for us to do, but there's no reason at least one or two of us can't do *nothing* with you. I know for a fact this family can be very good at watch and wait."

"Thank you." The truth was, after the events of the last two days, sole responsibility for the safety of Cole McIntyre was the last thing she wanted. She didn't think she could handle another life-threatening episode.

Sporting a satisfied look of the cat who had caught the canary, Violet rubbed her hands together vigorously. "I volunteer to make the sacrifice and help my cousin look after the hunky fireman."

All eyes turned to Violet, her enthusiasm a tad out of place. But then again, if there was anyone in the room to appreciate the delicate balance of life and find the ever-famous silver lining, it would be her cousin.

"Excellent plan," the General agreed. "There's safety in numbers. We shouldn't leave Lily and that young man alone."

Though it sounded like her grandfather was referring to tonight's effort to ensure Cole's good health, Lily had a feeling his choice of words had little to do with the recent scare and everything to do with their current plan of temporary cohabitation. Any moment she expected another lecture on no fraternizing among the troops.

Whichever he meant, she had news for her grandfather. He wouldn't have to worry about Lily and Cole being left alone. There was no chance on God's green earth that she was going to risk sticking too close to her patient and testing the doctor's theory of "third time's a charm."

CHAPTER TWELVE

Tonight was turning out to be a most interesting scenario. Cole was pretty sure having so many pretty women hovering over him was any man's dream. So far Violet had filled the air with some relaxing incense. Iris had just now shut her phone off after fielding multiple calls from a rather snooty woman grumbling about leaving her stranded without help the weekend of the biggest gala of the year. Cindy had left not quite an hour ago to check on a couple of animals recovering from surgery this morning. That left Poppy, Callie, and Lily together baking in the kitchen.

From the divine smells threatening to overpower Violet's incense, Cole had no doubt whatever came out of that oven was going to be loaded with calories, carbs, sugar, and taste like heaven. How not a single person in this family had a weight problem was beyond him. If fed a constant diet of Lucy's hearty, stick to your bones meals and Lily's fresh baked goods, he'd never again be able to race up the stairs in a burning building. Which was exactly why he'd been quietly exercising his ankle. Drawing the alphabet with his foot gave his ankle an easy workout. He'd made a mental note to find out about some weights so he could at least slow the atrophy that comes with an injury like this.

"If those people are so invasive of your spare time," Callie rinsed her hands at the sink, "I don't want to consider what it's like in the same house with them."

"There was a time when it didn't bother me at all." Iris slid onto a stool by the island. "Normally, she's very pleasant. Demanding, but pleasant. Things have been off kilter since the last trip. I think I've had enough. I've only been back at the lake for a few hours and already I can breathe again."

"Wow." Violet sat beside her. "Today was a lot of things, but relaxing isn't one of the words that comes to mind."

"No," Iris smiled at Lily just as her cousin met her gaze, "but home is home."

Cole had been fascinated watching the interactions between these women. It was obvious they were close. Very close. Anyone would have thought they were sisters. Or something better than sisters. He knew a lot of siblings who fought like cats and dogs.

"The secret to life is enjoying the passing of time." Lily shook something onto the baked goods in front of her and grabbed a plate, heading in his direction. "Doesn't sound like you're enjoying anything."

"No." Iris shook her head, snatching something from the top of the dish as Lily walked by, and bit into it. "Damn, I forgot how detrimental being around you is for my waistline. So good!"

"These are different." Poppy stood behind the small island, pilfering the stash left behind.

"They are." Lily waved the dish of brownies in front of Cole. "I tried the apple sauce."

Cole reached for a brownie and paused, looking up at her. Her cheeks flushed a dim shade of rose just before pulling the corners of her mouth into a smile. Maybe the baking change had been for him after all.

"Really? Apple sauce?" Iris stood to grab another from the pan. "These are fantastic and not a hit to the waistline. Beyond cool."

"They're not exactly dietetic." Lily set the plate down in front of Cole. He knew she was waiting for his reaction. "But it's definitely lower in calories and sugar than my traditional recipe."

Slowly, he took a small bite. Good. Really good. "Delicious," he mumbled around another bite.

Someone's cell phone sounded a notification. Callie the high school gym teacher grabbed another brownie and darted toward the door, pausing to kiss her cousin. "Have to run. I forgot I promised the new drama teacher to help with the play production."

"Man or woman?" Violet shouted to Callie's departing back.

"Woman," Callie called out, reaching for the door knob.

Violet shrugged shaking her head. "Can't win them all."

The conversation coming to a natural pause, one by one, each woman had a reason for taking off, leaving only Lily and Violet alone with him.

"You don't have to stay." Lily wiped at the kitchen counters. "He's doing much better."

She was right about that. His breathing had been just fine. The pain in his chest had eased to unnoticeable, and everything felt normal from the inside out. Heaven knew nothing felt normal from the outside in. If his buddies at the station could see him chowing down on brownies and cookies and chicken fried steak, they'd probably commit him to the psych ward for evaluation. Especially once they learned rather than gagging, he was actually enjoying himself.

"I don't think the General would be very happy with me if I left." Violet came to stand by him, bent to look in his eyes. "Stick out your tongue."

Cole felt his eyes widen with surprise as his mouth opened and he did as instructed.

"You look good to me." She straightened. "Do you mind if I go unwind for a bit in the other room?"

Lily shook her head. "Not at all. I'm sure all will be fine."

Violet snatched a brownie from the dish and waved it at her cousin. "You know, if you can get these to the point that you can call them diet friendly, this could be that item you've been looking for."

Lily glanced down at the dish and frowned.

"Want to share?" he asked.

She nudged the plate closer and Cole had to smother the urge to tease her.

"Not the brownies. What your cousin is talking about."

"Oh, that." She collapsed into the chair beside him. Today had clearly been a long day for everyone, but not till he noticed those few seconds of giving in to exhaustion on her face did he remember she had been awake and going nonstop since before the break of dawn.

Now he was torn between sending her off to bed for some much needed rest and learning more about the real Lily Nelson.

● ● ● ●

Lily wasn't sure she would ever get out of this chair again. Not till this very moment did she realize how bone weary tired she was. For a few seconds she considered reaching for a nearby blanket and curling up to sleep right here.

"Lily," Cole almost whispered. His voice floated over her like the warm blanket she'd been craving. "Hey. Maybe you should go to bed."

Her eyelids felt like they'd been nailed shut. Channeling all her energy to lift them slowly, her gaze settled on Cole, watching her with unexpected concern burning in his eyes. Wasn't that a switch? Until now she had been the one doing all the worrying about him.

"I need coffee." She shoved off from the chair. Lifting her feet seemed to take more effort than usual.

Cole flung his legs over the side of the sofa to sit up. "You need sleep."

"What do you think you're doing?" Her feet rooted to the floor, she blinked a few times before focusing on his good hand leaning on the sofa.

"I'm going to help you to bed."

"Excuse me?" Maybe he was having a relapse, because he and his sprained ankle were not making sense.

"You don't need coffee. You need rest."

"Well, I'm not going to get rest worrying about you hobbling around on a foot that's supposed to be elevated. Besides, I thought you wanted to know what Violet was talking about with the brownies."

He fell back onto the sofa. "Yes, I do want to know more, but I'd rather you sat down and gave yourself a chance to rest."

Even though she wanted to argue he wasn't the boss of her, his concern touched her more than she would have expected, and her tired body screamed, "for the love of God woman, sit down." She tried her best to sit gracefully, but flopped like a soggy Raggedy Ann doll. "Anyone who has known me for very long knows I love my work. I can't imagine not baking."

"I can see that."

"When I came home from Paris—"

"France?"

She nodded. "I went to culinary school there."

Cole whistled loudly. "Cool."

"Way cool. I arrived home by way of a brief stint working in

Manhattan full of excitement, eagerness, and dreams of opening my own bakery. My sister the bookkeeper sat down with me and helped work out a savings plan. Mom lets me live at the house rent free as long as the extra money goes into the bakery fund."

"Sounds like a nice nest egg is building."

"Not nice enough." She leaned back and kicked off her shoes. "Part of the business plan is a shop on Main Street."

"Here in Lawford?"

She nodded. "Like Iris said, home is home. I got to do a little traveling while in Europe. The distances aren't much more than the Northeastern states."

"See, there is an adventurous side to Lily Nelson."

She managed a slight shrug. "I suppose in some ways that's true."

"I don't know many women willing to venture out on their own through Europe or starting a business. Even making substitutions in recipes, is a bit of an adventure, don't you think?"

"Yes, I think." She couldn't help but smile. "But I also have seen the biggest and brightest cities in the world. Cooked in Paris and Manhattan. This is where I want to be."

His head bobbed. "I'm originally from suburban Massachusetts. Worked in the department there for a few years when a good buddy took a job up here. I came to visit him a couple of times, and a year later when the chance to work at the same department came up, I took it. No looking back."

"So you get it?"

He nodded again.

"The thing about the shops on Main Street in our little town is they don't turn over very often. Most of them have had the same ownership for as long as I've been alive."

"So it's taking too long?"

"Actually, it's happening too soon."

Cole shook his head. "I'm sorry, I don't understand."

"There's a small shop where the owner is retiring. Her husband passed away recently and apparently over funeral arrangements she told my mom she was thinking it was time to retire. It's a great location." Letting her head fall back, she heaved a tired sigh before straightening up again. "Besides the fact that I don't have enough money saved for the cost of converting a retail space into a fully functioning bakery, I still don't have the edge I would need to bring in tourists and residents from neighboring towns around the lake in order to sustain my business."

"Edge? As in..." the last word hung in silence.

"Something that is different from every other bakery in the county. I have a good reputation from my work at the Inn. Even so, it's not enough. There are lots of bakers who make delicious strudels and creampuffs and breads and you name it, it's delicious. I need that something special."

"Hence Violet's comments about a diet brownie." He nestled into the sofa. "Healthy, organic, vegan, keto, you name it, people are definitely more conscientious about the foods they put in their mouth."

"So I've noticed. They also go nuts over decadent sweets. Look at all the exclusively cupcake shops that popped up with icing as tall as the cupcake. Someone even managed to make a tourist destination out of raw cookie dough." In her pocket, her phone buzzed. A quick glance at the screen and she tapped the phone. "Hi Mom."

"Sweetie. Margaret O'Malley called. She's thought about it and wants to meet with you."

"I don't know." Even though she was dying to have a look at the back of the building. She'd been into the public storefront a million times growing up, but not the back, the space she'd need for the bakery. She sighed and shook her head. She didn't dare look at something she couldn't have. "The timing isn't right on this."

"Oh, Lily. The first step is always the hardest. I'll tell Margaret you'll be happy to meet her tomorrow morning at eleven."

Briefly Lily's mind drifted back to those first days after her dad died when her mom, putting on a brave face, shucked her apron and stepped into her husband's shoes at the funeral home. *First step.* "Thanks, Mom."

Cole shifted in place. "Seems, like it or not, you may be opening a bakery."

Like it or not. She definitely liked. And she certainly wanted. Her gaze drifted to the man stretched out on the sofa. Life was full of things people liked and wanted. Neither was her problem. No, she had a feeling deep in her gut that her greatest challenge just might be sitting in front of her.

CHAPTER THIRTEEN

Despite the stress levels of the last couple of days, Cole slept through the night like the proverbial baby. Though he would have liked to awaken to a considerably less swollen ankle, he had to admit it could have been much worse if Lily hadn't insisted he follow the recovery rules to the letter. At least the discomfort in his shoulder had gone from a constant thrumming to nearly nonexistent. As his grandmother used to say, "*a little bit of something is better than a lot of nothing*." He would take slow and steady progress over no change at all any day of the week.

Making his way into the bathroom this morning and dressing for the day went much more smoothly than yesterday, and certainly much better than the first night when he'd gotten stuck in his t-shirt like a toddler dressing for the first time. The one thing he did wish is that he wasn't still dependent on this stupid scooter for even short distances almost as much as he wished he could ditch the sling. Slowly maneuvering his way into the hall, the total void of human activity took him by surprise. The door to Lily's room, which yesterday had been ajar, remained closed this morning. He could hear the soft sounds of an ocean from the other side. No doubt Violet's contribution to everybody's peace of mind.

Even more of a surprise on his approach to the living area, was finding Lily on a stool, leaning over the counter, sleeping on top of multiple papers sprawled across the butcher-block surface. Careful not to make any noise and startle her, he looked over her shoulder. He was neither an accountant nor owned a business, but from what he could tell, she must have been up most of the night doodling with diagrams, lists, and enough math to make any normal person go cross-eyed. His chest tightened. No matter her bravado about timing and product, he could see from the number of pages crumpled, torn, scratched, scribbled, and sprawled in front of her, how very much she must want this.

The pages with the most scratching out were the ones with calculations. Ignoring the feeling he was intruding on a private moment, he held one page in particular. Estimated construction costs. With each item marked off down the list, the strokes grew stronger, bolder, and he would guess angrier. It didn't look like she'd found a way to make the math work. The basics were intact. Demolition, sheetrock, plumbing, electrical. All things that a building remodel needed and couldn't skimp on.

Had the talk last night of diet sweets given her one side of the answers she needed, and now the practical side of the plan was what had her falling asleep on the counter? As much as he hated to disturb her, he couldn't leave her here. She needed a little decent rest in her own bed before going to the meeting this morning.

Not till he tapped her shoulder softly and looked up from the counter did he notice the pile of pans and bowls in the sink. She must have baked something for the Inn. "Lily," he whispered.

She didn't budge.

"Lily," he repeated.

Her head shifted and she managed to bury her face deeper into the curved elbow of one arm.

"Lily, please. You need to go to bed." He brushed a lock of hair away from her face. She truly did look like an angel, especially with her eyes closed and her cheeks all pink from pressure against her arm. Despite his better judgment, he put his good hand on her shoulder and jostled it for a moment.

That seemed to get her attention. She mumbled, might have groaned, and very slowly lifted herself into an upright position.

"Hello, Sleeping Beauty."

"Sleeping?" Her gaze shifted to the clock on the wall. "Barb should be here any minute." With that, Lily sprang up as though she'd been awake for hours. From the fridge she pulled out a couple of trays covered with clear wrap. Then she hurried to the other side of the kitchen and loaded a shopping bag with more items.

"Don't you ever sleep?"

A soft rap sounded on the front door, and Lily whispered to him as she walked away, "Of course I do."

"Fooled me," he mumbled to himself.

From the chatter over the transfer of baked goods he concluded the Inn's guests were getting cinnamon rolls this morning with homemade icing. Just the thought of it had him almost salivating. What had she done to him?

"Feel better soon," the older woman called to him from the front door.

"Thank you," he waved back at her, and waited for the door to latch. "You should go take a short nap."

"That's the last thing I need. If I were to lie down now I wouldn't wake up till tomorrow morning." She walked past him and stopped at the sink. Sponge in one hand and dish soap in the other, she went to work at putting a dent in the mess she'd made overnight.

He wasn't convinced, but she did look like she had her second wind.

"You should be lying down with your foot up," she said a little louder to be heard over the running water.

"Yes ma'am." He almost saluted. "Are you still going to meet that lady this morning?"

"Yes. I think so."

"No more doubts?"

"Oh, I have plenty of doubts. Doubts, conflict, concern and poverty, but where there's a will there's a way."

The adventurous side of this nice girl was definitely growing on him. "Would you mind if I came along for the ride?" Before she could shut him down, he continued, "I could use a little fresh air and exercise."

"I understand the fresh air part, but I doubt seriously the doctor would agree with you about the exercise."

"On this contraption the only thing getting exercised is my good arm and my good leg. Besides, I'm curious. I'd really like to see what it is that has you so excited." He wanted to say controlled excitement, but figured that might get him in more trouble than not, so he opted to keep-it-simple-stupid.

"Why would you want to peruse an old boutique in a small town?"

He shrugged his good shoulder and smiled. "Hey, buildings are my thing. It's nice to work with them when they're not on fire."

"Work with them?"

"Yeah." He nodded. "A lot of us firemen do odd jobs. Our shifts are twenty-four hours long followed by forty-eight hours off. That leaves a lot of time with nothing to do between shifts. Besides, to be perfectly honest, we're not exactly paid the same as a CEO. The extra money is nice."

"Oh. That makes sense, I suppose." She stopped what she was doing and stared at him for a few long seconds. "You can come if you really want to."

"Great. I really want to." He didn't understand why, but being a part of this with her felt inexplicably important. Like it or not, he wasn't taking no for an answer.

● ● ● ●

From the moment she'd decided that for her own peace of mind she needed to meet with Margaret, her stomach had been center stage for a wild performance of tap dancers. No amount of Violet's aromatherapy or Cole's words of encouragement could put her or her stomach at ease.

If anything, the closer she got to the boutique, the worse she felt.

"Usually, on the rare occasion I drive through town, I'm not paying attention to the scenery." Cole kept his gaze focused on the passing buildings outside his window. "There's a lot of traditional charm on Main Street."

"Absolutely. It's the American dream. Anyone who lives here doesn't want to wake up."

"If only it were that simple."

And wasn't that the truth. In a perfect world, she would open her bakery. Money wouldn't be an issue, leases wouldn't be an issue, nor would customers. Her life would be like an animated movie. All the little creatures would help her bake, and knead, and roll, and cut the day's treats, and of course a fairy godmother would sprinkle them all with special powder, making every bite irresistible.

"You're smiling. Settling into the idea?"

She hadn't realized Cole had turned to face her. "Not exactly. I guess you could say I was gathering wool."

"From the huge grin on your face, I'd say you were gathering a lot more than just wool."

Chortling, she pulled into an empty spot not far from the boutique. "If you promise not to laugh..." She let her words hang waiting for him to nod. "I was picturing the bakery in animation."

"A cartoon?" His lips tilted upward in amusement.

"You promised not to laugh."

Even though his lips immediately flat lined, his eyes continued to twinkle. "Not laughing, but you have to admit, it paints an interesting picture."

"This is it." Pointing at the shop to her right, she sucked in a long slow breath and blew it out even more slowly.

"You ready?"

"No." She shook her head. "But I can't let that stop me."

Inside, the shop was pretty much as she had remembered. In the sketches she'd done for her "perfect world scenario" she'd done from memory. The rest she'd guessed from the outside of the building.

Cole seemed to be studying the room as intensely as she was. She could almost see him mentally sizing up the spaces, the distances, maybe even the repairs. "Do you think this is enough space?"

"Yes." She looked around one more time. Now more than ever, she was sure this would be the perfect spot. If only. "Picture it, a couple of café tables to this side of the door for those who want to sit down a moment and enjoy their pastry—"

"Will you serve coffee too?"

She frowned at the question. She asked herself that a time or two. "I can't make up my mind. Part of me says yes, extra income. The other part of me says no, more work. It also encourages people to linger and I don't know that I want them lingering inside. I think I just want them to come in and get what they want and leave room for the next person."

"I suppose I can understand what you mean," he said. "What else?"

Happily, Lily rambled on about colors and pictures and signs, and where to put the last cases a little past midway of the current shop. "And then," she waved towards the rear wall, "this wall would have to come forward a bit so this space and the current storage area will be the kitchen. Where the magic happens."

"If it's big enough?" he asked.

"Yeah," she nodded shakily, "if."

"I thought I heard voices." Margaret O'Malley came hurrying through the doors Lily had just pointed to. "I'm sorry, I was on a call in my office and I don't always hear the bell ring."

"No worries," Lily said with a smile. "This is a guest from the cabins, Cole McIntyre."

"How do you do?" Cole waited for the older woman to extend her hand. Lily wouldn't have expected the old-school gesture from him.

"Oh, yes." Margaret patted their already clasped hands. "The young man Lily keeps sending to the hospital."

Could there possibly be a stronger word than mortification, because right now Lily could feel the heat shooting up her body and burning strong in her cheeks. Of course, she should have expected this. In the small town the size of Lawford, most people knew everything about you, from your favorite color to how many times you wake up in your sleep to use the bathroom.

"I wouldn't quite say that," Cole defended.

"Really." Margaret let go of his hand and stepped back. "I see." She developed an odd grin before facing Lily. "Shall we get down to business, dear?"

"I don't know that there is much to discuss."

Margaret spun about and waived over her shoulder for Lily and Cole to follow. "Oh of course, you want to see the rest of the building. There's actually a lot more to it than you would think. I have quite a bit of storage." She walked through the doorway she had recently come out of and stopped dead center of a wide open space. "Years ago, my Herbie moved my offices upstairs. The second floor was originally an apartment, but I had no need for that. But I did need more storage. My Herbie, bless him, was so good at handiwork. I can't imagine doing all this alone from now on, but letting go can be just as hard."

Her entire life Lily had in one way or another flirted around the edges of death. She and her sisters had helped their mom ride the learning curve of wakes and funerals and dealing with the bereaved.

Still, finding the right words at a time like this came hard for her.

"But," an almost dreamy smile bloomed on Margaret's face, "as soon as your mother said you might be interested I knew moving on was the right decision. Herbie always loved eating your desserts at the Inn."

"Thank you."

Cole's gaze darted from point to point, zeroing in on a low beam midway between the walls, he gestured toward the ceiling. "Looks like your husband did a pretty good job. I'd say the joists run from front to back, which is why he added this crossbeam for support of the second floor."

Somehow Margaret's face seemed to glow even brighter. "Why, yes. He had wanted to hide it but that would've cost more money and it was only a storage room I didn't see the point." She continued walking. "Come along and I'll show you some more."

Together the three of them went from corner to corner, Margaret regaling Lily with stories from when she first opened her tiny shop out of her home at the outskirts of town, to moving here, to her life changing conversation with Virginia Nelson over funeral arrangements. Since the second floor had been used all these years for additional product storage, Margaret and her husband had installed a small service elevator that Cole was able to use to easily join them upstairs.

By the time the tour was over, Lily's head was spinning. Numbers and facts and possibilities were all tumbling around in her head. Every so often when Margaret stepped away to take a phone call or deal with a customer, Cole would lean in to give his opinion on the structural condition and possibilities for her bakery. Even though she would not own the building, Cole's contributions were going a long way to making her feel more sure of a trouble-free experience.

Lily struggled to wrap her mind around Margaret's offer to rent the space on a sliding scale for the first two years. Had her husband enjoyed Lily's baking that much? The option put an entirely new spin on her dreams. Just thinking about the possibilities for her future made her absolutely giddy. Her gaze drifted to Cole chatting sweetly with Margaret. A lot of things were making her nearly giddy today. Hopefully none of them would come crashing down around her.

CHAPTER FOURTEEN

"**A**re you sure you're okay? We were at the boutique longer than I'd expected." Lily watchfully walked along Cole's side.

"I'm doing much better." It was actually a bit surprising to him just how much better he felt not only after only a few days, but even since this morning. His shoulder wasn't hurting at all, and despite the swelling in his ankle, moving the joint in small exercises met with less resistance. In short, he was making progress.

Before they reached the door, Lily's steps slowed, taking in the voices on the other side. "Sounds like we have company."

"Does this happen a lot or is all this attention reserved for…special occasions?" He'd come within inches of mentioning his recent harrowing experiences.

The way Lily rolled her eyes, he thought he had his answer, but she responded verbally as well. "I'd love to say this is something special because I could have killed you—twice—but the truth is, they're fussers. All of them. And I love every one of them for it. Even if I can't imagine the General was this way in the Marine Corps, but then again…" She shrugged and shoved the door open.

As expected from the voices, the living room buzzed with activity. What wasn't expected was to find his buddies from the station dispersed among Lily's family. An appealing aroma smacked him in the face, making him sniff the air. "Is that what I think it is?" he asked.

Payton responded without looking away from the cards fanned in his hands. "Chili the way you like it. He's making enough to last you guys a week. We also brought the extra things you asked for."

"Found these fellas waiting for you." The General smiled at him. "Didn't think you'd mind if I let them in. Especially when they explained they would be cooking for you."

"No sir, not at all." If Cole had been injured anywhere else, these guys would have been at his side anyhow like white on rice.

Lily's grandmother looked up from her crocheted effort swooping yarn around a hook. She used the same hand to pat the sofa beside her. "I saved you a spot. Come take a load off."

Not until he'd heard those words had Cole realized just how much he wanted to not only sit, but put his foot up. "Thanks."

In order to help him get comfortable and elevate his leg, Mrs. Hart propped the sofa cushions under his leg and fetched a blanket for him from the other room. Cole didn't have the heart to tell her he'd rather relax in a refrigerator than under a blanket.

Payton chuckled under his breath, mumbling something about *molly coddled* before playing a card and carefully eyeing his partner Violet to see if he'd made the right move. When her turn came around and she played the ace to take the trick, Cole thought his friend would burst with delight. If it wasn't bad enough the guy could cream them all at a hand of poker, now he was going to add whist to his repertoire.

"I can't believe how good this tastes." Lucy swallowed the spoonful of chili. "No wonder you won first prize."

A friend she hadn't met before shrugged in a casual effort to hide how pleased he was with the complement.

Cole yelled over his shoulder, "That would be prizes with an S. Derrick's taken the blue ribbon every year for the three years that I've known him."

"Just don't tell anybody he uses ground chicken instead of beef. At most firehouses that's sacrilege." Payton tossed a card onto the table.

Lily pulled a glass from the cupboard and walked to the refrigerator. Holding the glass while it filled, she looked to her grandfather playing cards. "Where are Sarge and Lady?"

One thing Cole had noticed in the few days he'd been here, whenever the General was around, the two golden retrievers were at his feet.

"They are keeping Iris company on her walk," the General answered. "The best company when a person is wound as tight as she is."

"I do hope she can stay a while," Gram said without looking up. "She needs the lake."

"It has been a tense couple of years for her." Violet shifted the cards in her hand. "It will be nice visiting. What would be nice is if we could get all nine of us cousins here at the same time."

"Like when you were children." Grams smiled, stringing more yarn around the hook.

"What she needs is a good man." Lucy wiped her hands on a nearby dish towel, oblivious to the eye rolls the two cousins shared. "I need to get back to the house. Still have some chores to do and George is probably wondering where I ran off to."

"He's probably still at the marina. Bobby needed a second pair of hands fixing a hoist or some such thing."

Lucy turned to the fireman checking the big pot. "If you want to save this chili for your convalescing buddy, I'm making lasagna tonight. You're all welcome to join us for dinner. We're expecting a full house." She took a step back and didn't pause for a breath. "Have you met Callie?"

"Now, Lucy," the General's wife chided sweetly.

"What?" The housekeeper smiled impishly.

Smiling, Fiona Hart returned her attention to her crocheting. The moment Lucy closed the cabin door behind her, Lily and Violet rolled their eyes again and muttered a choral groan. Cole had to admit he got a kick out of Lucy's not so subtle hint.

"I swear." Lily shook her head. "She doesn't quit, does she."

"Who knows," Violet played a card, "maybe one day she'll actually set a couple up who are suited to each other."

"Fat chance," three voices echoed, including the General's. Every head in the room turned to face him.

"Don't look at me like that. It's obvious to anyone that Lucy hasn't got a talent for matchmaking."

"True." Violet set her cards down a minute. "She can sing every song from *Hello Dolly* from now until the next blue moon and it's not going to help her any. She's a lousy judge of compatibility."

On Violet's last word the house phone rang and standing closest, Lily grabbed it. "Hello?"

Unlike cell phones where a person could easily eavesdrop on a conversation, Cole couldn't make out who was on the other end, never mind who might actually be calling.

"Of course. No problem at all." Lily hung up and cast her eyes on the fireman closest to her. "Lucy says to tell you she's got some of Katie O'Leary's soda bread."

"You might as well give in." Violet shuffled the deck of cards. "She's liable to set the house on fire to get you guys in the same room with…" She looked up, frowning. "So is she trying to set up Callie or Iris?"

"Probably both," Lily muttered. "Unless there's some unsuspecting guest she's got in her sights."

"Heaven help the guest if she does." Grams wound more yarn more tightly around the hook.

"Is she really that bad?" Payton asked.

"Worse," the cousins echoed.

"Damn it." Derrick pointed out the window and spun around. "I thought you were kidding."

"What?" Lily looked in the direction of the main house. "Oh, Lucy."

Smoke poured out the first floor window of the white Victorian.

Gabe already had the fire extinguisher in his hands and was halfway to the door. Payton bolted to his feet and knocking his seat back, galloped out the door behind his buddy.

"Oh, my," Mrs. Hart muttered, quickly putting her project away. "Here we go again."

• • • •

Not that she'd know what to do, but Lily ran out of the cabin behind everyone else, shouting to Cole that she'd be right back. At least she had to admit if Hart House was going to catch fire, having three firemen within running distance was a bonus.

"We can't lose this house." Violet ran beside her.

Lily took in a deep breath. "We won't." This house had generations of memories and as much life in it as a living, breathing being.

Bolting up the porch steps, the sight of all three firemen in the entry talking to Lucy and the General, sent relief washing over them. Feathery waves of smoke still filled the room. Her grandmother and

Iris stood fanning the smoke away with magazines.

"I really am sorry," Lucy said softly. "I can't imagine how I could have made that mistake."

"What mistake?" Violet asked.

The General stepped forward. "Lucy thought it would be nice to start a fire."

"We figured that," Violet mumbled so only Lily could hear.

"She forgot to open the flue."

"In the fireplace," Violet spoke loud enough for her grandfather to hear and nod.

Lucy slapped her hands together and rubbed vigorously. "I'd better get back to the kitchen. Will you boys be staying for supper?"

One by one, each fireman shook their head, muttering, "Sorry, another time, rain check."

"I've got plans and we came in one car," Payton said.

Gabe held up the extinguisher. "I'll take this back to the cabin."

"Well, don't make yourselves scarce. There's always room for one or three more at the dinner or card table." Lucy turned to Grams. "Isn't that right?"

Waving her arm left and right in front of her face, Grams smiled. "Next time we promise to keep the smoke to a minimum."

"Yes, ma'am." Payton chuckled.

"I'll follow you back." Lily spun about. "I left Cole alone. For all I know, he's gotten up and is halfway here."

Sort of as expected, Lily found Cole off the sofa and on his scooter, but instead of on his way out the door, he was working his way back to the couch from the window. "I'm guessing since you guys are strolling home and I don't hear sirens, you were able to put it out?"

"Nothing to put out." Gabe returned the extinguisher to its place in the pantry. "Lucy started a fire but closed the flue."

"I see."

"She is right, there's a crisp bite in the air," Derrick offered.

"Uh huh." Lily turned off the burner under the pot. "Do you really have to leave or shall I dole out some chili?"

"Thanks," Payton smiled, "but we really do need to go. There should be enough there to last you a few days, even with the card playing crowd." He turned to face his friend. "I left your shirts and shoes in the closet with the rest of your gear."

"You sure you don't want to eat first?" Cole asked.

"Yeah, man. Behave yourself. We're on duty tomorrow, but will check in on you."

Cole nodded, and after a few more seconds of elbowing and teasing, the cabin was quiet as a church at midnight.

"Hungry?" Lucy asked.

"A little." Cole paused on his scooter at the coffee table. "Lucy might have had at least one good idea. It's a nice evening for a fire. Shall I start one?"

"No." Lily abandoned the warm pot of chili and met Cole in the living room. "You get off your foot. I'll go ahead and start it."

"Everything is all laid out and ready to go. I can do it."

"Yes, you can. But so can I." She inched in closer and reached forward, letting her fingers land gently on his arm. Words caught in her throat for an instant. "Please. I'd feel better if you let me do this."

His gaze bore into hers. For a split second she would have sworn he could read every thought and emotion swirling around inside her. Without moving an inch, he nodded, his eyes almost daring her to take the first step toward or away from him.

It took her longer than it should have. A magnetic force seemed to ooze from his every pore and pull her in. She wasn't sure if she'd ever felt so drawn to another human being before. There was no understanding it. All she knew for sure was that stepping back was her only option. "I'll get the fire started."

With a short nod, he took a wobbly step in retreat and she almost whimpered with regret. Once she gathered her wits about her, starting the fire came easily. Kindling and wood neatly stacked in cross rows allowing for air, she crumpled some paper to spread underneath and struck a match.

Flames burst upward so quickly, Lily sprang back. The sound of crackling wood mingled with the scent of pine needles George the handyman had most likely set underneath to ease starting. "Is there anything better on a chilly night than a warm fire?" she asked.

"It's definitely in the top five." Cole sank onto the sofa, his leg propped up nice and high.

And just like that the air in the room was completely back to normal. So why did her gut tell her on a scale of one to ten, normal just flew off the charts?

CHAPTER FIFTEEN

Down boy, Cole silently lectured himself. He'd come within a millimeter of kissing Lily. Common sense told him with the accident and mishaps, the situation was already more than complicated. He didn't need to add *fraternizing* to the mix.

Only his third day into recovery and Cole had pretty much all of sitting still he wanted. Even with this morning's outing to the storefront location, he was still antsy. Instead of lounging on the sofa like a Roman emperor, he'd rather be in the kitchen with Lily, helping her with the dishes, scooping out the chili, carrying it back here. "I've been thinking about the shop."

"You have?" An old shaker-style tray in her hands, Lily came his way with a huge smile across her face.

Scooting forward on the sofa, he let his injured foot slide to the floor and accepted the tray. "Thanks. And yes." The chili smelled fantastic, but it was the flaky roll to one side he noticed. "Did you bake these?"

"I did." Anytime anything to do with baking came up, Lily's expression always brightened.

"When did you have time?"

"There isn't much to ordinary buttermilk biscuits. I threw them together when we got home. Just tossed them into the oven not long ago so be careful, they're pretty hot."

She said that so matter-of-factly, as if everyone mixed up biscuits from scratch while doing a hundred other things. To most people biscuits in a can were as close to homemade as they would ever get.

The calories and carbs might kill him, but if he'd learned anything the last few days, he'd come to see life was too short not to enjoy every savory bite. The thought almost made him laugh. Only three days ago he would have balked at the amount of butter alone he'd consume with a single biscuit, never mind savor the prospect of one of Lily's home baked goods. "For what it's worth, I think the location on Main is perfect."

"You do?" Lifting the spoon, she flinched, a tiny wince escaping her lips.

"Are you okay?" He straightened in his seat, carefully watching her body language.

"Nothing. A little baker's stiffness. The downside of always leaning over to work on top of last night's paperwork marathon." Elbow bent, her fingers dug into the base of her neck. "I'm so used to it that I didn't even realize it until you pointed it out."

"Used to it?" He supposed his body was used to the occasional abuse his career choice put him through, but when his muscles protested, he noticed.

"I'll toss a bean bag into the microwave later. That and a couple of ibuprofen will help."

"That's not good for your liver. Come here."

"Excuse me?" Bright green eyes popped open wide.

"I could come over there," he scooted forward, "but you don't like it when I stand up."

"That's because nothing about standing follows the rules."

"And you always follow the rules?"

A slow grin teased one side of her face. "Maybe not."

"Then come here. I promise I won't bite."

Those sparkling green eyes widened again.

Some days he wished he was fluent in reading women's minds. Not bothering to say another word, he grabbed a cushion and tossed it on the floor in front of him, then gestured for her to sit.

Slowly rising from the chair, Lily looked as though she'd been asked to walk the plank. Taking cautious steps across the small space, she turned her back to him, then eased onto the cushion and leaned against the sofa.

With his good hand resting lightly on her shoulder, he pressed carefully with his thumb, searching for the out of place tightness.

"Oh, that does feel good."

"I'm glad." Very glad. Gliding and pressing, going from one shoulder to the other and back, he kneaded the kinks in her neck much the way she might do with a mound of dough. Her left side definitely held more tension than her right. One strong push of the pad of his thumb and he felt the hard knot at the same moment he heard Lily's sharp intake of breath. "I'd say I found the spot"

"Oh, yeah."

Now he wished he'd thought to ask her to grab a bottle of lotion. His gaze fell on a small vial of essential oils Violet had left him. He'd already forgotten what it was, but it couldn't hurt. Lily's neck fell forward and pausing briefly, he reached for the little bottle. "Loosen a couple of buttons on your shirt, please."

Her head tipped to one side, allowing her a brief sideways glance in his direction.

"So I can get some oil on your neck and rub a little deeper," he explained.

Letting her chin fall back against her chest, she undid one button and he thought might have mumbled something like, *too bad*.

"Are you going to take Mrs. O'Malley up on her offer?" Distraction was key right now. He needed to get his mind on something besides Lily's soft skin under his fingertips.

"I am so very tempted," she mumbled.

She wasn't the only one. "The building is in solid shape. It wouldn't take much work to implement some of those sketches you showed me."

"Maybe not much work, but plenty of money."

"I may be able to help with that."

"Oh." Her head tilted sideways again.

"I'm guessing I know a few guys who might be willing to trade a little hard labor for a year's supply of baked goods." He chuckled. "You may know one of them. I believe you were briefly engaged."

"A year huh?" She smiled and her head fell forward again.

"Yes. From…what will the name be?"

"What name?"

"Of the bakery. Your bakery."

"The Pastry Stop." Somehow she seemed to relax even more with the words. "It's kind of simple. I'd thought about something with Patisserie but decided that might be a little too pretentious for Lawford."

"I like it. It's perfect. I'd want to stop."

This time she twisted at the waist. "Would you?"

"Of course.'

"No, really. Would you drive out of your way for a croissant? A Danish? A cake?"

"Well, I haven't had your Danish or cake but I've had enough of your baking to truthfully answer yes."

"And that's the rub. I can't bring in every resident on Lawford Mountain in order for them to taste my baking and know it's worth the drive."

"Well—"

"I need one item. One thing that stands out in a crowd. That will make folks talk about me and drive from across the lake to shop with me instead of their own town bakery."

"That shouldn't be so hard. I've tasted your baking and your cooking. You're not bad." A grin split his face. Even though she couldn't see him, he hoped his teasing tone came through loud and clear.

"Gee thanks." Under his fingers, her shoulder rose and fell with a stifled chuckle.

"You're welcome." The knot in her neck was loosening to the point that he probably didn't need to keep rubbing at it, but he liked working on her shoulders. Knowing he was helping. Making a difference in her life. Admittedly a very small difference, especially one handed, but he liked it nonetheless. Who was he kidding? He liked being anywhere near Lily. Hell, he even liked being in the middle of nature with sketchy cell reception, no decent TV or internet—and with her. And wasn't that a riot. Her spitzenbuben cookies weren't the only addictive thing around here. Three days ago he could hardly wait to go home and now, well, now he wondered how long could he safely milk a sprained ankle.

● ● ● ●

If anyone doubted there was a heaven, all they would need is five minutes with Cole's hands working away the stress of the day and they would become a true believer. Lily had no idea how long she'd been under his touch, but she did not want to move. Ever.

"You never mentioned." She tried not to purr as his fingers shifted to rub along the edge of her spine. "Did you always want to be a firefighter?"

"No." He pressed lightly at a tight spot. "I was going to conquer the monetary world in my original plans. I have a degree in economics."

"Really?" She leaned a bit to one side in order to get a look at his face. He seemed perfectly serious.

"Really." He motioned for her to sit back. "I lasted one year behind a desk and knew I had to find something else."

"But firefighting?" She turned around, greedily hoping he wouldn't stop his ministrations. "Not the first thing that comes to mind with a degree in economics."

"That's what my grandfather said."

"You have one of those too? The kind who always has the answers?"

"Yes, and he's a lot like yours, but Navy not Marine. He's a ring knocker too."

Immediately she recognized the nickname given to military academy graduates. "Does he live near here?"

"Nope. My dad's the one who comes from generations of northeasterners. Mom met my dad in college and since she didn't really have a hometown, I grew up near Dad's family. My grandmother never cared for winter, so when my granddad retired they settled in Florida. They're happy as clams."

"How did you wind up a fireman?" Back in full massage mode, her head lolled from side to side.

"I came within inches of taking another office job. Instead of a cubicle this one at least came with a window. Before I'd fully made up my mind, a few of us had gone on a weekend fishing trip. We were caravanning in three cars. Halfway to our favorite fishing hole, we saw smoke and realized a house up the road was on fire. We'd left late so it was pitch black out. One by one we pulled over in front of the house. Everyone ran in different directions. At first banging on the door to wake the family up and make sure everyone was out, then grabbing hoses to do what we could until help arrived. We were in volunteer fire department country and knew help wasn't around the corner. By the time the fire truck arrived, I was hooked. The adrenaline high of saving a family of five and their dog was like nothing I'd ever felt before."

"I can't even imagine." The only thing she'd ever saved from burning was a batch of cookies.

"What about you?"

"Me?" She turned for a better view of him and leaned against the sofa as his hands slid away. "What about me?"

"I'm guessing you've been planning for this bakery for a long time."

She nodded. Long time was an understatement. She'd been in charge of her own kitchen since that first Easy Bake Oven. In the beginning, staying in Paris had an irresistible charm. The cafes, the lights, the river Seine, and the buzz of places like the famed Latin Quarter and Montmartre were amazing for a small town girl. Briefly she gave New York City a chance. In the end, it hadn't taken long for her to realize the only charm she wanted—or needed—was right here at home. "I've been saving for years."

"And you have to have the bakery right on Main Street?"

"That's the dream."

"How many locations have come available since you started saving? I would think in such a small town there would be at least some turnover."

"Nope. None." Pulling her legs tightly against her, she rested her chin on her knees.

"So what you're saying," his brows crinkled above a pensive gaze, "is this is a one time shot?"

Was that what she was saying? Was it now or never? At least never on Main Street. And just how important was having a bakery on the prime shopping road in town? The road that linked a dozen more small towns just like Lawford. The one tourists drove through while hunting for the perfect summertime play spot, exploring foliage in the fall, or en route to ski down a snow-covered mountainside. "Have you ever wanted something so badly you can almost taste it?"

"Hasn't everyone?"

"Once I moved back to Lawford, to save money I moved in with Mom. I've studied under some of the best pastry chefs in the world. I practice new recipes on my family whether they like it or not—"

"I'm sure they love it," he interrupted.

Yeah, they probably did. At least Lucy complained enough about her waistline. "But can I do it? Really do it? No one else to fall back on. Just me and my pastries. Deep down," she heaved a sigh, "I don't know."

Her own words surprised her. She'd never admitted that to herself before, saying it to a near stranger was almost as startling as hearing her fears voiced out loud. Cole slid off the sofa and sank onto the floor beside her. His good leg tucked against him, aligning with hers, their knees bumped and her breath caught.

"Every time I rush into a burning building, for a flicker of a moment," he pinched his thumb and index finger in front of her then let his hand fall to his side, "my mind acknowledges this could be the last time. This could be the time the fire wins. The time I don't come out alive."

Even though they barely knew each other, her chest actually ached at the thought of losing him.

"But another part of me, the smarter, stronger part, recognizes that I could be someone's only hope of survival. And not because I'm a fireman, but because I'm a good fireman. I love what I do and that shows every time I turn out for work."

She let her chin tip up and back. "I bet you're damn good at it too."

"So are you." A slow lazy smile slid across his face. "I'm not sure you realize just how good."

"I suppose good enough for a marriage proposal." Even if his buddy had made it in pure fun.

Dark as steel, eyes reflecting the fire's heat leveled with hers. A pop from the fireplace sounded and neither bothered to look. She couldn't have dragged her eyes away from him for her own sainted mother. His head tipped to one side and she knew in that instant he was going to kiss her. And she couldn't think of anything she wanted more.

Lips soft and strong barely brushed against hers. The fingers that had kneaded away the tension of the last few days threaded with hers. Her eyes drifted closed and her breath caught in her throat. If the world stopped now, she wouldn't complain. But the world didn't stop. Only his kiss. As slowly as he'd eased against her, he pulled away.

Hesitating only inches from her face, he blinked. "Should I apologize for that?"

Most of the air in her lungs stuck in her throat, all she could do was slowly shake her head.

A tiny smile pulled at the edge of his lips. The lips that had just given her the sweetest, gentlest kiss she'd ever had in her entire life. "Any chance you want to do it again?"

She hadn't a clue if kissing him again was a good or bad idea, but at this moment, she was pretty sure she didn't care.

CHAPTER SIXTEEN

The distant humming of an alarm broke through the haze of sleep. Not a hum, a buzz. Actually, a phone. Her phone. Lily flung her arm out to grab her cell from the night table, stretching to reach over her pillow.

"Here you go," a deep voice rumbled really close to her ear.

Both her eyes shot open. Not a pillow. *Cole.* Cole on the floor, propped against the sofa, smiling down at her. His bad wrist resting against her, the other holding out a buzzing phone.

"Thanks." Shifting to an upright position, she sifted through the mental cobwebs of her mind in an effort to put this morning's pieces together. The only problem—this close to a living, breathing, hunk of a man—who definitely knew how to kiss—her mind was putting very little together. There was no forgetting the fabulous massage, or the breathtaking kiss, and then they talked. *That's right.* For hours they shared stories about her grandfather, the Marine Corps general, and his grandfather, the Navy Captain, their childhoods, likes, dislikes. Story after story, they were always stunned at how different their lives were and yet how much they still had in common. The last vivid memory she had was being tucked into his side, sharing the color schemes for the bakery of her dreams. Somewhere between the champagne cream walls and the retro tin ceilings, she must have fallen dead asleep.

"Are you going to answer?"

Lily looked over at those deep gray eyes and wished desperately that she had a cup of coffee, or ten, because at the moment her caffeine deprived brain could not care less about the phone. The buzzing stopped, only to begin again. This time she looked at the name—Hilltop Inn—and bolted upright. "Oh, no. I didn't take the kalockys to the Inn. "Barb, I'm so sorry."

"What?"

"I have kalockys. What time is it?"

"Just after seven and I'm not calling about my guests. I threw sugar and cinnamon on toast and heated yesterday's leftovers. So far, this weekend's crowd hasn't noticed."

"Gee, thanks." Nothing like being on the precipice of major financial investment and realizing all that's needed to replace her is a loaf of store bought bread and some cinnamon.

"You know I didn't mean it that way. Anyhow, I just got a call from Nan Elizabeth at the Lakeside Resort. They've ordered desserts for all their catered events from Sam at Dough's for ages, and you know your baked goods are better than Dough's."

Keeping her eyes on Cole, maneuvering his scooter in the tiny kitchen, she nodded, though it didn't matter. Barb couldn't see Lily, the woman kept right on talking.

"Sometime last night Sam collapsed in the kitchen. His wife got worried when he stopped answering his phone, went over, and found him sprawled on the floor. Hospital said if she'd waited another thirty minutes to check on him, it might have been too late."

It took Lily a few seconds to take her mind off the now brewing pot of coffee Cole had started and process the words collapsed, hospital, and too late. "Oh no! Is he all right?"

"Should be. It's a wonder what they can do with a burst appendix. But Nan has a bigger problem."

What could possibly be bigger than almost dying?

"In all the hoo ha, no one noticed the refrigerator door wasn't shut."

Barb didn't have to explain further. "How long?"

"There's no telling how long he'd been down before his wife found him, but at least eight hours that we know of."

Whatever had needed refrigeration wasn't going to be pretty after that many hours above minimum temps. "Too long," she mumbled.

"Exactly. Whoever steps in now is going to have to start from scratch."

The hairs on the back of Lily's neck stood on end.

"Governor Thompson's favorite niece is getting married tomorrow night."

"Did the cake survive?" Pulling out the red vinyl stool, Lily sat at the island, her gaze on the still gurgling coffee pot.

"Italian Buttercream icing. What do *you* think?"

Nope.

"*And*," Barb dragged the single syllable word out, "a Venetian hour."

"Oh man." This was getting worse by the minute.

"I've texted you the quote. It says what they ordered, and how much of it they ordered."

"Texted me?"

"Yep. You're it. You've got about thirty-six hours to put together a killer dessert presentation for the governor's favorite niece."

Cole appeared, setting a steaming mug of caffeine in front of her. "How many guests?" she asked.

"Four hundred. Give or take."

Four hundred? Had Barb lost her mind? Not even with the entire pot of coffee and the Inn's professional kitchen could she pull off a Venetian Hour for four hundred guests without serious help. "I may be good, Barb, but nothing about me is faster than a speeding bullet. I'm not Superman."

Sliding onto the seat beside her, Cole mouthed "yes you are" with a straight face.

"What about Gerty in Pinefield?" she asked.

"Nope. She's already committed for a fiftieth anniversary party for some Boston tourists."

Her mind scrambled to think of bakers big enough and close enough to pull this off. "Allison at Sweets to Eat. Didn't she just take on more people?"

"She did. She also had to shut down the kitchen when a plumbing repair uncovered asbestos. Like it or not, you're the best option."

"You mean the only option."

"Lily, honey, you pull this off and people will be raving about you from here to the Atlantic. Don't worry, I'll help."

Taking a quick glance at the items on the order, Lily shook her head. Barb had no idea what this would take. And thirty-six hours and one little baker weren't going to cut it.

• • • •

The way all the color momentarily drained from Lily's face, Cole feared she might keel over. The woman who'd refused to take no for an answer, insisting on caring for him, and who'd juggled her personal and business world around in order to stay at his side, seemed to have run into what looked to be an insurmountable obstacle. He couldn't imagine what.

"Give me a few minutes to inhale some caffeine and I'll call you back." Lily tapped her phone to disconnect and began scrolling quickly, then back, then again more slowly. With each pass, the creases in her forehead deepened. By the third pass her head shifted from side to side and her lips were pressed into a thin line.

"That bad?" Noticing she had yet to take even a single sip of coffee, he nudged the warm brew closer to her.

Without looking up, she curled her fingers around the handle and gulped a long swallow. The cup back on the counter, she blew out a sigh and shook her head again.

"Want to share?"

Tossing her phone on the island, she wrapped both hands around the nearly full mug and took another long gulp. "Making multiple desserts for a crowd of four hundred takes time. Or at least a large team of bakers and a huge facility."

He nodded. "Makes sense."

"I have neither."

"Okay." He hadn't really heard enough of the conversation to fully put the pieces together yet.

"It's crazy."

Again, he nodded.

"Insane."

He could see the wheels in her head turning. "Superhuman."

"Or Superman?" Her scowl of a response had him biting back the grin teasing his lips.

Her gaze lifted to the tiny oven behind him and then out the window into the distance. From the direction she stared, his guess was her grandparents' house. The impressive, porch-wrapped, white

Victorian structure that stood as a testament to strong family bonds.

"I gather," he ventured, "your boss' help won't be enough."

Lily huffed a curt laugh. "Barb is just fine at turning an oven on and maybe even unwrapping a pan of frozen pastry, but a baker she will never be or I'd be out of a job."

"Maybe that's all you need." Hurrying up with his thought as her narrowed eyes threw daggers at him. "Helping hands to load and unload trays, grease pans—which, I will mention, I am pretty darn good at if I do say so myself—transfer pastries from pan to dish—"

"You're volunteering?" The crease between her brows took on a more quizzical form, but more importantly, the gleam in her eyes was slowly returning. She had an idea. He could almost see it forming in the back of her mind. "We'd need more ovens," she muttered, more to herself than to him.

At this point he figured silently nodding would be more helpful than breaking up whatever train of thought was building momentum.

"And more hands. But hands with some skill."

"Lucy?" he dared mention.

A bright grin was his reward. "Lucy and I bet Katie O'Leary would help. That woman definitely has the bakers touch. Poppy isn't bad with a spatula, either."

"You do have an awful lot of family. And if I'm not mistaken, there are an awful lot of cabins with ovens and not that many guests."

Her chin dipped briefly as she retrieved her phone and scanned the list again. "We might have to do a few substitutions. The warm fridge may have ruined much of the prep work, but should not have affected the gum paste roses." Her face brightened. "If Sam has already made those, I might even be able to put this cake together." This time she lifted her face to meet his. "If I have help, that is."

"Of course. I can do a lot one handed. And I can't lift anything heavy, but my fingers work just fine on the not so good hand."

"You mean broken." She smiled, shook her head, then chuckled. "You know, I really think we can do this."

"I know."

"You do?"

"Uh, huh. I figured it out the minute you told me the idea was crazy and insane. You had that exact same look in your eyes when you told me that I was staying put and you were taking care of me."

Her brows buckled again. "Well," the creased forehead smoothed, "I suppose I didn't have a clue how I would make it all work then either."

"See?"

A slowly growing smile made her eyes twinkle. He liked that. A lot. Probably more than those cookies that he found almost irresistible. Much like her. And wouldn't that put a crimp in his plans.

• • • •

"If you ask me—"

"I'm not." Fiona Hart cut her housekeeper off. She loved Lucy, more than a sister, but some days she was just a tad too eager to marry off all the single women of Lawford.

"Well, we've got a handsome as Adonis, strong as—"

"*Luucyy.*" Fiona didn't look up from her crocheting. Every time she did, somehow she wound up with longer or fatter stitches.

"Okay. Can I at least say single?"

What was the point in reeling the woman in? Fiona had spent her entire adult life handling a Marine general, she didn't have it in her to do the same with her matchmaking housekeeper. Even if she'd yet to make an actual match.

"Haven't you ever heard of confined space romance? This is the perfect chance to set the stage for love. Some candlelight. Soft music. Wine. But no. Blasted grandfather has people in and out of that house like a stampeding herd of cattle."

"You've never seen a stampede, have you?" Not that Fiona was an expert, but she'd had to mingle with a local or two over a thousand years ago when they'd been assigned briefly at the joint base in Texas.

"Yoo hoo." Rapping on the door, Katie O'Leary popped her head in the back entry and nudged the door open with her hip. "Since I'd be coming this way anyhow, thought I'd save the General a trip to the One Stop for the loaves you ordered."

Fiona glanced up at the clock. "Shouldn't you be at the store manning the cash register?"

"Fiona Maureen, how can I be in two places at once? I've got everything Lily asked for in the car. Could use a hand unloading."

"Lily?" Fiona and Lucy echoed, both frozen with confusion.

Mary Kathleen O'Leary straightened her shoulders and tucked her chin tight against her long neck. "Now what would you two be staring at," her Irish lilt showing, she clapped her hands, "there's work to be done."

Without a moment's hesitation, Lucy dropped the pan she was scrubbing and Fiona jumped to her feet—not a thought for her yarn or stitches—and followed their friend and shopkeeper out the door.

"Grams," Lily called from a few feet up the hill, "phone's off the hook again and you're not answering your cell."

Fiona leaned into the van for the groceries Katie held out. "That's because it's on my night stand."

"Grams," Lily whined much like she did when she was five years old and her mother told her it was time to put away her Easy Bake and get ready for bed. "What good is having a cell phone if you don't have it with you?"

"Strikes me as plenty good." She hated those dang contraptions. Seemed like few people remembered how to talk to real people nowadays. The number of times she'd see couples on a date and both with their noses in their phones, she wondered why they'd bothered leaving the house at all.

"I got everything you asked for." Grinning from ear to ear, Katie handed off a couple of bags to Lucy, then Lily.

"I can take a couple." Cole rolled to a stop in front of Lily.

Katie's gaze lifted, and starting slowly from the top of his wavy brown hair, descended past his broad shoulders, continued down to the knee resting on the scooter, and drifted back up again. "Oh, I'd say you could handle a lot more than that."

"See," Lucy snapped at Fiona. "That's what I've been saying!"

Rolling her eyes and shaking her head, Fiona ignored the banter and turned to her granddaughter. "May I ask what this is all about?"

"It's why I called you. I need some help." Lily sucked in a heavy breath. "Heaven help me. I've—no—we've got less than thirty-six hours to bake and feed a near army."

Fiona watched her granddaughter march up the porch stairs. What the heck was she talking about?

CHAPTER SEVENTEEN

"Where are the pecans?" Poppy lifted the kitchen rag on her left, moved the package of parchment paper, then looked once again to her right.

Licking blended cream cheese from the tip of her finger, Lily swallowed and smiled. *Just right.*

"Aren't those for the pumpkin tartlets?" Lucy asked.

"Nope, turtle cheesecake bites."

"That's right." Lucy snapped her fingers. "Caramel drizzle and candied pecans."

Poppy fisted her hands on her hips. "And Katie needs more pecans."

"Are you sure she doesn't have all the bags?" Lily asked.

"Right now," Poppy shook her head, "I'm not sure of anything other than my feet hurt."

Bless her family. Everyone had dropped their own lives and responsibilities to come help. Callie wasn't worth a damn in the kitchen, but her enthusiasm helped when it came to running back and forth from cabins to the house whenever anyone needed something and for cheerleading extraordinaire. Cindy was still stuck at the clinic but promised to do a grocery run for any additional supplies needed when she was through. Planning for twenty dozen of this and twenty dozen of that, the wedding coordinator must have expected each guest to eat their weight in desserts. Poppy was doing a great job at measuring out ingredients and even mixing a few items. She'd been a huge help with the filling for the crème brulee tarts. Only ten dozen more of those to go.

At least the caterer was doing his share. He'd offered to torch the tops on site so they wouldn't have to deal with the timing on that. Merrily humming away the song 'Just Leave Everything To Me' Lucy monitored the chocolate molding. Lily's cousin Iris had left early this morning, heading back to work before her boss became totally apoplectic. Violet returned to Boston on Iris' heels. Not wanting to disrupt everyone's lives, Lily opted not to let them in on the current chaos or she knew they would have changed their plans. Her cooking team of six, soon to be seven helpers was working out just fine.

"I don't know about you," a tray of gluten free tartlet shells in each arm, Callie leaned into her cousin and whispered, "why does that song in particular always make me nervous?"

Whispering back, Lily leaned closer. "You don't suppose the use of courted, dated, wed, marriage, and consummated in one song could give any single woman the heebie-jeebies?"

"And here I thought it was the unpleasant picture of 'torso pounded' that bothered me." The two women laughed softly as Callie carried the trays out the door and across the drive to the Sycamore Cabin for baking.

"Well foo," Poppy frowned. "I'm positive I only took one sack full to the cabin."

"Is someone looking for this?" Grams held up a large grocery sack bulging with smaller bags of pecan halves.

"Yes," Poppy squealed. "Where was it?"

Grams pointed to the floor by her yarn bag. "Not sure how but it wound up in there. Good thing pecans weigh more than yarn or it could have been a while before I noticed."

"Here you go." Katie walked in the door, kicking it shut with her foot and balancing a large plastic tub as she walked. "Just finished stirring up the last of the pecans and have them waiting to go in the oven and another batch set to cool. Can't do anything else without more pecans."

"Is that what I think it is?" Lily's chest tightened with nerves. She'd given the job of glazing the pecans to Katie because the woman swore her grandmother's method was the best. She trusted Katie in the kitchen, but giving up control gave her her own case of heebie-jeebies.

"Earlier batch cooled and ready for your approval." Katie held the tub with one corner of the cover lifted up.

It was like reaching into a black hole. Would this work or not? Would they be great or not? Lily had been tempted to cheat and do a quick sauté and higher temperature bake for shorter cooking time. It would have worked, but Katie was right—slow and easy was always better. Bringing the candied pecan to her lips, she slowly set it on the tip of her tongue. Immediately, her cheeks tightened into a happy grin. "Perfect."

"Of course. My granny wouldn't dare let any of us down." Katie scanned the kitchen quickly. "Where's that hunky fireman?"

"It was decided the best thing for our progress was to send the General away. It's Cole's assignment to keep him busy for a few more hours."

"He can keep me away any time he wants." Katie wiggled her brows and shimmied in place. Maybe they'd been pushing too long and too hard, but every woman in the place broke down laughing.

"You'd better keep your mind off Lily's fireman—"

"He's not my fireman," Lily huffed.

"—and on those pecans!" Lucy finished without skipping a beat.

Katie rolled her eyes and shut the lid on the pecans. "You have to know I'm teasing, Lucy. I wouldn't pilfer Lily's fireman—"

"He's not my fireman," Lily repeated a little more loudly

"What I don't understand," ignoring Lily's whiny input, Katie continued, "is how Cole is out with the General when he's supposed to be off his feet."

"Special dispensation," Grams called from her seat. "Besides, Lily's young man gets around so well on the scooty thing that I'm thinking it might be nice to have around here."

"He's not my young…" Lily let the words fade away. What was the point? No one was going to believe her, and after last night, maybe she didn't believe herself either.

●   ●   ●   ●

Every moment spent with the General, Cole fought the need to stand at attention. The man was friendly and even funny, but no matter how many jokes he told, the air around them crackled with the words: Retired Marine General.

"Does anyone know Floyd's real name?" Cole asked softly of the man across the checker board from him. Most residents of Lawford Mountain knew the barber shop story. Due to its parallels with the nineteen sixties sitcom, Floyd's barber shop had a reputation that kept people coming through the doors. When Floyd sold it years ago, the owner not only kept the business name, he adopted the owner's name for his own.

The General shook his head. "Nope." With a big grin on his face, Lily's grandfather jumped over several pieces and took the last of Cole's pieces. This was the fourth game in a row he'd lost. Either he was worse at checkers now than when he was five years old, or he was incredibly distracted. Considering his mind had been on Lily, last night and this morning, wondering how her day was progressing, and batting around ideas for her dream, distraction hit the nail on the head.

"Doesn't look like she almost killed you." Floyd's words drifted over his customer's head.

Once again, thinking of Lily, Cole had lost the thread of the conversation.

"Twice," the General added. "Would have thought my girls had more sense."

Floyd's hands froze mid snip. "Twice?"

Seated nearby kibitzing the checkers game, Ralph leaned forward. "Poisoned him."

"She did not." The words came out more harshly than Cole had intended. "I'm allergic to sesame."

"See." Ralph sat back. "She poisoned him."

"It was not her fault," Cole defended.

"But she did run you down with her car?" Floyd looked at him over the rim of his glasses.

"She did not run me down." Not exactly. "I sort of hit her car."

Lifting his gaze from the board, the General's eyes narrowed. "*You* hit her?"

"Sort of." He hadn't expected folks talking about Lily like she was some kind of incompetent klutz to bother him so much.

"Sort of," the General repeated. Something in the way the man studied Cole left him uneasy.

"I was jogging in the dark," he explained. "Early in the morning. Very early."

The General continued to stare.

"Well, if you ask me," Ralph closed the magazine he held in his hands, "no matter how you look at it, you're lucky to be alive."

That was true in more ways than one. Not in terms of getting away with only a few inconvenient injuries, or overcoming his allergic reaction, but being here and now, in this time and place with Lily Nelson. Yeah, for the first time in a long time, he'd say that was especially lucky.

The next few games flew by much the way the previous ones had, the General wiping the board with him.

Floyd brushed the neck of his last customer, placed the cash into the old-fashioned ornate register, and smiled. "That's it, fellas. Time to close up and go home."

Cole hadn't heard a word from Lily nor had anyone at the house reached out to the General. Following the cliché *no news is good news*, he had to assume all was well. What he didn't know was if it was a good time to return. "What do you say if we take a little stroll down Main Street?"

The General shook his head. "Not with that foot you're not."

So distracted, Cole had actually forgotten about his injuries. "I can roll down the street?" His levity fell flat on the older man.

"It's time we get home to check on the women." The General pushed to his feet.

Cole nodded. What more could he say or do? Like a good soldier, he covered the short distance to the car, slid into the seat while the General stowed his scooter, and debated whether or not to interrupt Lily with a text.

"I understand you went with my granddaughter to look at the shop." The General pulled the car onto Main Street. "What do you think?"

"I think it's a great location."

"Mm," the General grunted.

"It would be a shame if she didn't grab the opportunity."

"Mm," the General repeated.

"After all, she's a great baker." Cole wondered how much more could he say to carry this conversation all the way back to the house.

The General cracked a smile. "That she is."

Silence hung as they approached the section of town near the potential bakery.

"So, you think she can do it?" The General slowed the car as he drove by.

Cole nodded. "I do. It will be easier with help from her friends."

The General looked to him and raised a single questioning brow. "Which friends might those be?"

At this point he wasn't quite sure what would be the correct answer, but it was definitely safe to say if nothing else, he and Lily were now friends. "Me, for one."

"For one?"

"Yes," he nodded. "I'm pretty handy with power tools."

"Mm," the General grunted again and Cole couldn't decide if that was a good or bad thing.

"And," he continued, "my buddies at the firehouse. Everyone has a specialty."

The older man didn't say anything. Pulling to a stop, he put the car in park, dropped his hands over the top of the steering wheel and stared up at the soon to be vacant building. "All I've ever wanted is for my daughters and now my granddaughters to be healthy, productive, and happy." His head bobbed. "As I put on the years, and things…change, happy seems to tip the scales."

Cole nodded, unsure if he should speak, wondering what *things* had changed.

"My Fiona is my world." He continued to stare at the building in front of them. "Made staying alive worthwhile so I could come home to her. Did a better than fine job of raising our girls. Oh, I was home from time to time, but all the credit for the women they are goes to my Fiona."

Again, Cole nodded even though the man wasn't looking at him.

"I would hate for any of my girls to pick the wrong man. A man who didn't believe in them."

Even though Lily's grandfather wasn't looking directly at him, Cole had the distinct feeling this momentary walk down memory lane was very specifically aimed at him.

"Of course, as long as God's willing, any man who doesn't do right by her will have to answer to me." Now the General leaned straighter and turned to face Cole. "Though I might let his own grandfather have a crack at him first."

Before Cole could respond, the General had turned away, shifted the car into reverse, and pulled onto the road. For some reason, Cole had the distinct impression something very important had just happened between them, but for the life of him, he couldn't quite put his finger on what exactly just went down.

CHAPTER EIGHTEEN

Scanning her surroundings, Lily took in the different workstations in her grandmother's massive kitchen and dining room and smiled. They'd accomplished a lot. She'd been on her feet all day and feared if she sat for even a moment's rest, she'd never get back up again. "I'll put these in the fridge in the Sycamore Cabin and check on Katie."

"Good thing I thought to thaw a couple of casseroles." Lucy dried her hands on her apron. "Not going to be cooking supper in here tonight."

Callie yawned. "I'll set the tables on the veranda. Dining room is otherwise occupied."

Anything that hadn't needed to be refrigerated was left on the dining room table to be packaged for transport. Mostly the chocolate and pecan cookies.

"Did anyone remember to tell Cindy to pick up corn syrup?" Poppy set a clean pot back on the stove. The number of items that required warming, melting, or blending over a fire had kept them steadily cleaning pots and pans all afternoon.

"I did." Wielding her spatula with the practiced precision of a woman who had been doing this for hours, Grams moved the gluten free shells for the pumpkin spice tartlettes from the cooling rack onto a freshly washed cookie sheet.

Everything was coming together. Lily's cheeks lifted with satisfaction. She hadn't been all that sure she could actually pull this off and if her calculations were correct, she was actually ahead of schedule. Enough so that she might be able to catch a few hours sleep tonight. That was if she could actually get any sleep. Despite the last-minute stress, this entire situation had her feeling more excited than she'd been since packing to leave for Paris.

With the refrigerators at the main house already full, she lifted the tray of cream puffs to take to another cabin for storage. She'd only taken a few steps when Lady and Sarge took off from their corners in the kitchen, practically sliding across the kitchen floor toward the front door. Clearly, the General was home. Her heart did a little jig. If her grandfather was home, so was Cole. And that tugged the satisfied smile on her face into a full-blown grin. Had she ever been happier than this very minute?

"Whoa." The General came to a stop at the kitchen door. "You have been busy."

Cole came rolling up beside him. His gaze immediately landed on Lily. Eyes twinkling, the corners of his mouth tipped upward in a familiar smile. Her heart stuttered before continuing its happy dance.

Her mind drifted back in time, to last night and the way her lips tingled against his, then to this morning curled up safe beside the man currently grinning at her like she'd hung the moon. As happy as she was in her element baking up a storm, the truth was, what had her happier than a pig in slop right now wasn't the chance to prove herself to the resort and the governor's guests, or the chance at the bakery of her dreams. Heaven help her, she was more than happily falling in love with the man she'd almost killed—twice.

"Hi," Cole said from across the kitchen.

"Hi," she murmured back.

His gaze shifted to take in the surroundings. Remnants of powdered sugar and flour floating about, piles of pans and baking sheets, and a handful of women scurrying over one thing or another, the place must look a mess to him.

"Need some help?" he asked.

Dogs at his side, the General shook his head. "I don't think this kitchen will ever be the same." Without waiting for an answer, he took a step closer to his wife and planted a brief but branding kiss on her lips.

"Might as well make yourselves useful." Lucy waved her arm in the direction of the side veranda. "Callie is setting the card tables for supper. Why don't you both go see what she needs."

The General nodded. Tapping his toe behind him, he did a full military turn and walked back into the hall. Both dogs on his heels, he almost collided with Katie.

"Oh, excuse me, General." Katie took a step back and looked up at Lily. "Fridge in my cabin is almost full. How many more trays do we have?"

Lily held up the one in her hands. "This is the last one for now."

"Great. I'll take it." Katie retrieved the tray of cream puffs.

"Hurry back," Lucy called over her shoulder. "We'll be stopping to sit down for dinner in a couple of minutes."

"While normally I'd be drooling over a chance to break bread with all you fine people, my feet and back are begging for a comfortable chair and a good ole Irish Coffee."

"Oh, of course." How foolish of Lily not to have suggested Katie go home after she'd helped with her secret pecan recipe. The turtle cheesecake bites had turned out to die for, and then Katie had moved on to helping with the cream puffs. Lily could just stab herself with a fork for being so inconsiderate. She reached out to retrieve the last tray of cream puffs.

"Don't be silly, girl. You've still got plenty to keep you busy. I'll just be putting this in the old fridge and then going along my way. Whistle if you need more help tomorrow." With a wink and a dimpled grin, Katie whirled around and out the door.

Suddenly, for the first time today, Lily didn't know what to do with herself. Turning in place, she caught sight of Cole still grinning at her, and her insides warmed from her pounding head to her toasty toes. At least one thing was perfectly clear to her momentarily addled brain. Standing in the middle of the kitchen staring at her fireman was definitely not the right thing to do. *Her fireman.* Another grin threatened to take over her face. She really liked the sound of that. *Her fireman.*

● ● ● ●

Something had shifted and the last thing Cole wanted to do now was analyze the bejeesus out of how he felt.

"You," the General leaned back, a hand scratching the top of each dog's head, "should go to your cabin and get off your feet."

Cole refrained from the obvious retort of "I am off my feet." Technically, he had not been on his feet all day—his knee, yeah—but not on his feet.

"He's right." Callie stood, picking up the dirty dishes. "Moving about all day is going to set your recovery back."

There was no sense in arguing. His foot was feeling much more inclined to agree with her than it might have been earlier this morning, and yet he didn't want to leave Lily with so much work still to do. Not that there was much he could do to help. Actually, nothing at all he could do. With this stupid scooter, he'd only get in the way.

"We'd better get back to work." Poppy stood. "There's more to do."

Somehow, in the bustle of the Hart clan clearing the table, dealing with dirty dishes, and Lily sorting through another round of checklists, Cole found himself propped in an easy chair with one of the General's murder mysteries. A comfy chair that Lily had insisted on dragging into the kitchen when, after a good ten minutes of debate, he'd refused to go home and lie down. Several added cushions kept his leg resting up high. The best it had felt for hours.

Watching whirlwind Lily was amazing. The second nature with which she whipped, beat, folded, molded, and kneaded fascinated him. She moved around the kitchen like a dancer on stage. Elegant and fluid. Sure, he'd seen her putzing around the kitchen at his cabin, but this was different. It was a little window into what her world would be like when she ran her own bakery.

Hands on either side of her lower back, Lucy stretched left then right. "I think it's time for another pot of coffee."

Lily looked up, almost as though she'd forgotten Lucy was even there.

"Oh, that sounds wonderful." Callie rolled her shoulders.

At that moment, Poppy came in the door from the dining room workstation carrying two trays stacked precariously in her hands. "This is the last of my batch."

All heads glanced up at the large analog rooster clock over the sink, but it was Lily's eyes that popped open. "Oh, wow. I didn't realize how late it is." She dipped the last of the mini éclairs into the chocolate and set them on the tray. "This is a good place to stop for the night."

Lucy stretched and leaned. "Works for me."

"What's left I can handle in the morning—"

"You mean we." Callie propped her hands on her hips and the others nodded their agreement.

"We." She smiled. "But there's just a few last minute touches and the oatmeal cookies should be it."

"Oatmeal?" Poppy asked.

Lily shrugged. "Apparently it's an eclectic group."

The order had been taped to the refrigerator doors for all to see. Every so often Lily would pause and look it over and scribble on the margins. By now anyone helping knew exactly what had been done and what was missing.

"If you ask me someone fell asleep at the wheel deciding on the cookies. I mean," Lucy rolled her eyes, "Who orders frosted malt-chocolate cookies and then throws in oatmeal raisin?"

"The Governor's niece," multiple voices said in unison.

"I'm with Lucy." Cole set the book aside. Not that he'd actually read much. "They should have gone for something special like your spitzenthingy cookies."

"Spitzbuben?" Lily supplied.

"Yeah." Cole smiled at the mere memory of the sweets. "They're absolutely the best."

"You know," Lucy waved a hand at Lily, "you did make a double batch the other day. I bet if you gifted the wedding with some extra cookies, no one would complain."

"And lots of people would be introduced to your cookie!" If he could stand on his own two feet, Cole would have kissed Lucy for the idea.

The way Lily's eyes widened under crinkled brows, he didn't think she agreed with either of them. "If you hadn't been gone with the General most of the day I would have said you've spent too much time near the hot ovens."

"It's a good idea," he said.

Poppy wiped her hands on a rag. "He may be onto something. If you substituted the spitzbuben—which, he's right, are out of this world—for the oatmeal they might get upset, but who complains about an extra something for free."

"Spitzbuben," Lily repeated more softly with less incredulity in her voice. Slowly, the crease in her forehead eased and she repeated, "spitzbuben," followed by the corners of her lips curling upward. Nodding her head and grinning contentedly, she settled her gaze on Cole. "Spitzbuben, it is."

And there he had one more thing that made him incredibly happy with no good reason why. Except maybe one. Lily. But he already knew that. What he didn't know was how long would it take for this to wear off. Had he ever been this completely contented by the mere sight of another woman? Nope. Not a one. So much to consider.

It didn't take much longer for the kitchen to be lick-the-floor clean and for Lily and him to be on their way back to their cabin. And wasn't that another thought that made him want to grin like a fool. A lot of things made him want to grin lately.

"If I weren't covered in layers of sugar and flour and ground nuts, I think I could easily collapse into bed right now and sleep for a week." Lily undid the top button of her baker's uniform. "I'll be right back."

"I've probably got residual dustings on me too." He followed her down the hall and smiled at her soft chuckle.

"Things were a little crazier than usual."

"But it was fun watching you. I think you'd be crazy not to take that lady up on her offer for the Main Street locale."

"Mm," she muttered, turning into the second bedroom.

Thanks to the shirts Payton had brought him, changing for bed had not been another ordeal like that first night. Dressed in a worn out flannel button-down shirt and sweatpants, he looked at the scooter beside the bed. He'd really had enough of rolling around on that thing, but standing on his own two feet simply wasn't an option, no matter how much the swelling had gone down. *Maybe.* He'd have to see how everything felt in the morning. Perhaps with this orthotic boot he could manage with the aid of a cane or walking stick.

"You ready to hit the sack?" Lily popped her head in the doorway.

"Not sleepy yet. Thought I'd hang out on the sofa and see what's not on the TV."

Lily's eyes twinkled with amusement. "Two minutes ago I could barely hold myself up and now, well, I seem to have caught my second wind."

"You're not going to keep baking, are you?"

"No." She shook her head. "What's left can wait till tomorrow. Thank heaven it's not a morning or lunchtime wedding."

Despite preferring to walk on his own steam, Cole shifted onto the scooter and waved for Lily to lead the way.

By the time he made it to the sofa she was already prepping and pounding the cushions for him to recline.

"Uh." He cleared his throat. Funny how he suddenly felt like a nervous teen. "I'd rather just sit with my leg on the coffee table."

"Oh." She stopped mid cushion-patting to look at the table.

He cleared his throat again. "With you."

Her head snapped up and her gaze shot from him to the sofa and back before a small smile slowly appeared. "That would be nice."

Once she had him comfortably installed on the sofa, she insisted on making her specialty garlic parmesan popcorn before snuggling in beside him. This was nice. Very nice. He didn't even care what was or wasn't on TV. Leaning into his good side, she fit perfectly.

"Oh, look." She waved the remote at the TV. "*Return To Me*. I love that movie. Is this okay?"

Not that they had much of a choice with the limited TV offerings, but even though he'd never heard of it, if she liked it that was good enough for him. "Sure." By the time the dog on screen was at the door missing his favorite master, Cole had pegged it for the chick flick that it was, and that was perfectly fine with him. Everything about tonight was fine. Even when she fell asleep against him less than midway through the movie—that was fine. And the funny little squeak she made that some might call snoring, that was fine too.

Despite his physical challenges, his life had never been more fine. Deep in his gut he knew he didn't want to give this up. Brushing a loose lock of hair away from her face and tucking it behind her ear, he let his thumb run down the side of her face. His angel. Gentle and strong, kind and tough, sweet and adventurous. Perfect. Definitely did not want to give this woman up. He wanted to watch old movies, fall asleep snuggled, help fix her bakery, encourage her dreams—be in her dreams.

He almost laughed at himself. Until this week his life and career plans had been clear. Marriage and children were not for him. Excellence in firefighting depended on a clear head. On his ability to arrive on the scene and focus on one thing—saving the strangers inside. A wife and family would only be a distraction. There was no time in a deadly fire to worry about getting home for dinner, making it to the school play, or one day dancing at your daughter's wedding. No, a clear head from a no-strings life was the cornerstone of his career. Until now.

CHAPTER NINETEEN

Waking up in a man's arms was not something Lily should let herself get used to. Definitely not a good idea. A terrible idea. Worst ever. Only a few more days and Cole would be heading home. But boy did she want to stay right here till the cows came home—especially with never having seen a cow anywhere near Lake Lawford.

Exhaling a soft breath, she eased out of Cole's grip and made her way to the bathroom. As quietly as possible, she showered, dressed, and shouldn't have been so surprised to see Cole by the stove fixing breakfast.

"It's going to be another long day and you'll need some protein to keep you going."

"Thanks." She watched him flip the sides of the cooked egg over a cheese filled center. The omelet slid easily out of the pan onto the plate. "I'm impressed."

He set the dish down in front of her. "I'd be drummed out of the fire station if I couldn't hold my own in the kitchen."

For just a brief moment, Lily allowed herself to consider how many other things he no doubt *held his own* at.

"Drink this too. It's good for you." He set a glass of green frothy liquid in front of her.

Instinctively she leaned back. "Do I want to know what's in that?"

"Good stuff." He grinned and continued whisking another bowl of eggs.

She eyed the drink suspiciously. After all, she'd seen all those green powder containers that had been on the counters. "I don't suppose I could have a cup of coffee first?"

He shook his head. "Nourishment first. Coffee second."

Not till he tipped his head toward the steaming pot behind him did she realize he'd made her coffee too. That would be another thing she could get used to. Someone else brewing coffee and making breakfast. No, not someone. Cole. The least she could do was taste the off-putting concoction. Pulling on her big girl panties—so to speak—her hand stretched forth, and closing her eyes, she took a hesitant swallow. Not what she'd expected. Holding the drink away from her, she examined the glass more closely. Nothing very informative. The drink was green. Waving it under her nose, she frowned. Definitely banana. "What is in this?"

"Not bad, huh?" He slid his eggs onto a plate and scooted around the island to sit beside her.

Smiling she took another long sip. "Not bad at all."

"Not everything that's good for you has to taste bad." Smiling, he stabbed at his eggs.

"Fair enough, since not everything that's supposedly bad for you tastes good either." She chuckled, thinking about her grandmother's efforts to make meringue cookies. The simplest recipe in the world for pure sugar overload, and yet somehow at her grandmother's hand they always came out tasting like a doorstop.

Cole dangled his fork mid air. "Bon appétit."

"Bon appétit," she repeated, taking in a forkful of her own. The eggs were fantastic. She'd never known anyone who could make them so thin without a crepe pan. "These are wonderful."

"Enjoy, because I have a feeling once we get back to Hart House, you're not going to have any chance to eat again."

Wasn't that the truth. She'd rather have everything delivered to the resort and out of her responsibility sooner than later. Shoveling down the final bite and swallowing the last sip, she stood and hurried the dishes to the sink. "I'll let you know as soon as we're done."

"No," he scooted up beside her, "I'm coming too." Before she could utter an objection, he raised his hand. "I'll stay out of the way, but I'm coming."

She wouldn't object. She wanted him there with her, if only for moral support. Nodding, she took a quick look around for anything she was forgetting.

"Your phone." He held out her pink case clad cell.

"Oh. Thanks." So immersed in bakery thoughts, she would have left the dumb thing on the counter.

"You go on ahead. I'll be over as soon as I get into some clean clothes." He lightly touched her arm, handed her a travel mug of warm coffee, then followed her down the hall.

Everything in her felt lighter. She could tell it was going to be one helluva day. Even the short walk to Hart House seemed quicker. She'd have sworn the big old house winked at her as she made her way up the front porch. Pounding feet came hurrying down the main stairs. Violet.

"Didn't expect you back so soon." The porch door slammed behind her.

"The new heating system is stuck in air conditioning mode. No one likes relaxing in an arctic blast." The cousin who always managed to look like she'd just enjoyed a relaxing day at a beachfront spa frowned a long moment before plastering on a typical smile. "Why tough it out when I could be with my favorite cousins here. Notified all my clients, did a load of laundry, and drove back late last night."

"Well, if it isn't one thing it's another."

"The joys of living in an old building." Violet's smile twitched as she fell in step with Lily. "Grams filled me in on the situation and I'm here if you need more hands."

Along with not expecting to see Violet, Lily hadn't expected to find all her sisters already up and waiting for her at the kitchen island. The second thing to hit her was the strong smell of coffee. Anxious to come over, she'd not taken a sip from the mug Cole had given her. "As soon as I finish this one," she held up the cup, "I'll take the rest intravenous."

"Get in line." Callie took a long sip from the mug cradled in her hands.

Sliding very slowly off the chair, Poppy took a few stiff steps before making her way to the counter with the coffee pot. "I think I've been run down by a steam roller."

Lucy winced tying her apron behind her. "I think I have muscles that have never been used before."

"How long were you guys working yesterday?" Violet asked.

The sisters' gazes bounced back and forth from one to the other before Callie finally said, "Long enough."

"And I suppose you guys didn't stop often enough to stretch?"

Violet said.

"We didn't stop at all." Lucy refilled her coffee cup.

Grams came through the doorway, her step not as light as usual.

"You too?" Violet blew out a sigh. "What would you people do without me?"

The array of surprised and horrified looks on all her family's faces made Lily want to laugh. Violet could indeed be a little disconcerting at times, but she was right about one thing—life just wouldn't be the same without her. Good family and now good…friend. What more could a girl ask for in life?

• • • •

Feeling so much better this morning, Cole was terribly tempted to ditch the sling and use only the walking boot to head across the way. Only two things stopped him. Deep inside he knew pushing too hard too early was never a good thing, but the key reason he would use the scooter and keep the sling had everything to do with the green-eyed redhead and not wanting to annoy or disappoint her. Another first for him. Other than his grandfather and parents, he didn't much care what anyone else thought of him.

Hart House sat perched near the top of Hart Land. Property that sloped gently down to the lake. A smattering of small rental and family cabins dotted the landscape in between. Built on a slope, several steps lead to the wraparound porch at the front but access from the rear of the house sat level to the ground, making it easy for him to roll onto the porch and up to the back door.

Laughter and giggles carried from the kitchen, growing louder and clearer as he made his way to the door. Despite the heavy workload yesterday, that same laughter, giggles, and even teasing had abounded. He looked forward to another day with all these people.

"That's it," a soft voice carried. "And again."

Cole pulled the door open, and getting better at maneuvering the scooter and juggling doors one handed, he crossed the threshold only to come to a full stop. He'd expected to see people bustling about, flour and powdered sugar covering things already. Someone by the oven, another at the counter, maybe even someone with their head in the fridge. Nothing in his time here with the Hart family prepared him for the sight in front of him.

"Up, down, up, down. Atta girl."

Lily, her sisters, her mother, her grandmother and Lucy were scattered about the kitchen. Elbows pinned to their sides, palms parallel with their shoulders and facing skyward, they bobbed up and down like colorful pistons. The Oompa-Loompas from Willie Wonka's chocolate factory had nothing on these ladies.

Their ringleader—Violet. "Remember. Stand tall, like a string is pulling at the top of your head," Violet's voice practically sang.

If the room full of women bending up and down at the knees was an unexpected sight, Violet stole the show. Hands flatly together above her head, one foot against the other knee fanning out like a chicken wing, Violet balanced on one foot. He couldn't decide if she looked more like a prima ballerina. Or a cross between a Tibetan statue and a pink flamingo.

Two dogs raced through the doorway and into the kitchen, both plopping their hind quarters on the floor. Seated, turning their heads from side to side, they took in the show. Yeah, Cole understood exactly how they felt.

Hands clapped, and the General stood at the back door. "Picked up the van Sam is lending us. Let's get this show on the road." In a matter of seconds, bodies dispersed every which way.

"We'll load what's in the fridge and dining room here first," Lily waved an arm toward the back hall, "then hit the stash at the other cabins. Cindy, you and Poppy get started on the new stuff."

"How many trips do you think it will take?" Cindy reached for a couple of bottles on the island and pulled them toward her, unscrewing the caps.

Lily stood by the fridge. "I haven't seen the van but I'm sure more than one."

"Payton has a van he uses when doing handyman work. Shall I give him a call?" Cole liked the idea of having something more to contribute, than merely cheering them on.

"Let's see how the first load does and if we need it, you can call while I run it over. Don't want the resort staff to botch any of the refrigerated items before the caterers get there."

"Like these?" Callie set a tray of creamy looking tiny tarts on the island.

"Exactly." Lily placed a second tray on the island beside them.

Grinning like a cat with its fill of fresh cream, Lucy came out of the walk-in pantry. "This is so exciting. I've been waiting to try this thing out on some crèmes needing brulee."

"Try what?" Cindy spun in place to look at Lucy, and her eyes popped open wide.

"No way." Lily waved a hand. "The caterer is going to do that."

"Well pooh." Lucy huffed. "Not that it matters. Dang thing is stuck."

Lucy continued to push on a large red button at the top of the small pastry torch and everything in Cole had him ready to ditch the scooter, fly across the room, and yank the thing away from her.

With a loud pair of barks, Sarge and Lady must have had the same thought. The two dogs bolted, paws scrambling underfoot against the slippery tile, and whizzed past Cindy.

"Oh, hell." Cindy lost her balance and the open bottle in her hands poured all over the floor. "What a me—"

"Whoa!" Lucy cut her off. Taking a blind step back from the dogs, her foot on the fresh puddle went one way, her other foot the other, her arm flailed, and sure enough, the torch lit—the curtains.

"Aah," a very loud voice screamed, and from one side of the room Cole could see Fiona Hart running with a spray bottle in hand.

"Where's the fire extinguisher?" Already having quickly scanned the walls, Cole hadn't spotted it. He needed to get the fire out before Mrs. Hart made matters worse if that bottle didn't contain water.

"The pantry!" multiple voices shouted.

A blonde, a redhead, and a brunette collided at one side of the island. Three women screamed "I'll get it" and practically knocked each other over before straightening, pointing at each other and screaming "go help Lucy" then, once again, crashing into each other on their way to the pantry.

Normally Cole would have been at Lucy's side helping her up, concerned with injuries, but there was no time for that or dealing with the frantic women bouncing off each other like a couple of rubber balls.

"Everyone out!" the General ordered. Doing his best to help Lucy up without succumbing to the gooey mess on the floor, his wife almost skated past him and the gruff older man's voice boomed "Out" again.

Moving slower than he would have liked if he weren't in an orthotic boot, Cole raced to the pantry, grabbed the extinguisher, and thanked the heavens it was a professional model and not a mini household kitchen variety.

"Clear," he shouted to Lily, batting at the rapidly burning curtains with one of Lucy's full-length aprons. "Now," he yelled louder, just as the apron lit up in flames. "Damn, it. Drop it." Not able to wait, he pulled the pin and sprayed the curtains, the dishrag on the counter that had lit up, and to his relief, the apron she'd let fall from her hands.

"Oh, my God." Color drained from Lily's face. Her hands drifted to cover her mouth.

Dropping the extinguisher in the sink, Cole maneuvered around Lucy and the General now on their feet, and pulled Lily into his arms.

Her head dropped against his shoulder and he felt understanding dawn in her shivering shoulders.

"It's okay," he murmured.

"Thank you." The General's beefy hand slapped him on the shoulder. The man took a step away and Cole heard his heels snap together. "Attention!" the patriarch bellowed and Cole could have sworn he heard spines snap straight. "We have a mess to clean up and an order to deliver. Let's get a move on."

Even Lily pulled out of his arms, sucked in a breath, and reached under the sink. Pausing, rags and cleaners in each hand, her gaze locked with his, and sweet lips softly muttered, "thank you."

Just like that everyone in the room was back to business as if this chaos was any other normal morning in the life of the Hart family. Except for the fire, none of this was anything close to normal for his life, and he was pretty sure normal for him had just taken a dramatic and permanent shift.

CHAPTER TWENTY

"Are you sure you don't want to stay and see how it all looks set up?" the caterer asked Lily.

As much as she would love to see the final display and the guest's reactions, at only a little past noon, this had already been the longest day of her life. "Thanks, but it's all yours."

"Oh good. I see everything is here." The wedding coordinator waltzed past the stainless-steel counter where the cookie platters had been set. Coming to a complete stop at the button-sized spitzbubens, she did a double-take. "These aren't on the menu."

"No." Lily swallowed. She'd hoped not to be here when someone noticed the addition. "They're a special family favorite. A little gift to compensate for the last-minute baker change."

The young woman hugged a computer tablet closer to her chest, and eyes narrowed, pointed. "May I?"

"Of course." In hopes of hiding her nerves, Lily tightened her lips into a smile.

If there was such a thing as real time slow motion—the woman's arm stretching forward, her fingers uncurling then gripping closed around the cookie's edge, that same arm lifting back toward a now open mouth, and the tiny confection slipping inside—was definitely in very-slow-motion. Even slower, jaw muscles moved up and down, chewing, tasting, and from the sudden gleam in her eyes, Lily would bet savoring.

"Oh, my," the coordinator mumbled, hand to her mouth. "*What* are these?"

"Spitzbuben."

The woman's eyes circled round as she reached for a second cookie and popped it into her mouth. Chewing slowly, she swallowed and nodded. "I don't care what they're called. If the rest of your desserts taste as good as these, I'm recommending you to every client we have. Do you have a business card?"

"Uh." *Card?* "Not on me."

"What was your name again?"

"Lily Nelson."

"I mean your bakery."

"Oh," and just like that her mind was apparently made up, "the Pastry Stop."

Well penciled brows creased to a point. "Doesn't sound familiar. Where is it?"

"Lawford. It's uh… under renovation. Today was a special effort to help Sam."

"Well, I'm sorry Sam was hurt but am delighted to meet you." She eyed the plate of cookies, pressed her lips tightly and slowly inched back. "These things are addictive."

Lily couldn't help but laugh out loud. "So I've been told." By a very special someone. A someone she wanted to be the first to know that she would be accepting Margaret's deal and officially opening The Pastry Stop. Though from the raves, maybe she should call it The Spitzbuben Stop.

"You ready?" Her grandfather stood, keys in hand, behind her.

"Yes. Let's give these folks room to do their magic." Lily's long day suddenly felt a whole lot lighter. The only thing she wanted now, more than anything else, was to see Cole. To tell him her news—at least—about the shop. Her other revelation, that she had tumbled chef hat over heels in love with him, would have to wait. Maybe after they got the shop together, enough time would have passed for him to feel at least a little the same.

"You look happy." The General smiled at his granddaughter. "You should be. This wasn't an easy feat."

"It would have been a whole lot worse if Cole hadn't been there."

"True. Those extinguishers aren't light. Even injured, he didn't disappoint." General Harold Hart lifted his chin and pointed to the door. "The van is around front now. Out of the way of the caterers. My car is parked at Sam's. Once we switch out you can get home and get off your feet."

"Oh, that does sound heavenly." Especially if it could involve a warm fire, a soft sofa, and *her* fireman.

• • • •

"I'd like to say you shouldn't have done that," Violet brought a fresh ice pack and set it on Cole's shoulder, "but seeing as how you single handedly saved Hart House, and maybe Lily too, I'm glad you did. Just sorry about the arm."

"It's only a little sore. No big deal."

"And the foot?"

He used his good hand to wave it off. "That's what these boots are for."

"Right." Taking a step back, her hands on her waist, Violet shook her head. "So now what?"

"Excuse me?"

"If you can walk across a kitchen on your own steam and wield a thirty pound fire extinguisher, you probably don't need a live-in nursemaid."

Oh, hell. That hadn't occurred to him. "On second thought, my ankle is really throbbing and, and, maybe the shoulder needs another adjustment."

"Uh, huh." Laughing, Violet slapped his good leg and backed away. "Thought so."

"Thought what?"

"Just, *so.*" Violet tipped her head toward the door. "That sounds like the General's Jeep. I'll hitch a ride and do my best to make sure he doesn't bring the evening card brigade over here."

"That won't be—"

A squeaking hinge announced the opening door.

"Sure it won't." Violet shook her head and waved at him. "I'll see myself out."

"Oh." Lily came to a stop in front of her cousin. "You leaving?"

"Yep. The patient is in good hands now. He's all yours." Violet leaned in to kiss Lily on the cheek and closed the front door behind her.

"What's she so chipper about?" Lily asked. "A couple of hours ago everyone looked like Raggedy Ann left in the rain."

"I could say the same about you. Well, not the Raggedy Ann

part, but the chipper part. You look much too happy for someone who should be dead on her feet."

Lily headed in the direction of the club chair and Cole patted the sofa beside him, delighted when she pivoted in place to change direction. He wanted to feel her close. Especially after what Violet said about his time together almost being over. Logic said in less than a week he shouldn't care so much, but who said logic had anything to do with love.

"Wow." Lily kicked off her shoes and practically fell into the seat beside him.

"Come here." He shifted slightly away, dropped a pillow behind her and lifted her feet onto his lap. Using only his good hand, he ran his thumb under her arch. "Tell me what happened."

Lily burrowed into the cushions. "Keep this up and I won't be able to utter a word."

"Try." He smiled.

"Well," she adjusted the cushion to sit a little straighter, "you were right."

One brow shot up a little higher than the other. "I was? What about?"

"The cookies. The shop." She laughed. "Everything."

Everything. Oh how he wished that included his recently adjusted views on love and logic. "Care to explain?"

"I'll start with the cookies. The wedding coordinator tried one. Actually two. She loved them. Wanted my business card."

"I won't say I told you so." All that mattered was that soon the world was going to know how great a baker Lily was.

"Thank you." She rolled her eyes and almost purred as his thumb pressed deeply into her tired feet. "I'm going to call Margaret and tell her I'd like to sign a lease on the building."

"You are?" His hands froze.

A huge grin took over her face and her head bobbed. "Yeah, thanks to you."

"Me?"

"Without you here these last few days, I probably would have passed on even going to look at it, on taking this last minute job, and even if I had accepted, sneaking in the cookies."

"I don't believe that for a minute." His fingers resumed their motion. "You're made of much stronger stuff."

Her head tipped to one side. "You really think so?"

"I know so." He patted her foot and shifted to the other. "There's a difference between recognizing obstacles, and money is definitely an obstacle, and being afraid to tackle said obstacles."

"I don't know. Maybe it's just having you around that brings out the best in me."

"I was nowhere on the scene when you packed yourself up alone and went to study in France. That was a very brave thing to do. I certainly wasn't around when you drew up your first business plans. Not everyone can do that either. And I'm not the one who orchestrated an extended family into a successful catering order." He shook his head. "As much as I would love it to be true, you don't need me."

"You do?" Her head lifted off the pillow and her gaze grew more intense.

He wasn't totally sure he understood the question, but it didn't matter because the truth was when it came to Lily, for him everything was yes. He nodded.

Her feet slipped out of his lap as she pushed herself upright beside him. "Just to be clear, are we talking ego here?"

Cole shook his head. "Far from it."

"And you used the word love and need in the same sentence?"

This would be the time when a block of nerves should lodge in his throat but they didn't. His only concern was that admitting the words love and need were very much the way he felt about her might be enough to shove her completely off the sofa and out the door. "I did."

Silence hung while Lily quietly stared at him.

"It's your turn to say something," he said softly.

"I'm waiting for you to backpedal. You know, explain why this isn't how it sounds."

Something popped in her eyes. A glint of anticipation. Maybe even hope. But nothing that said she was preparing to run for the nearest exit. Some things were too important to rush, to risk, to chance, but his gut told him if he didn't answer now this would be the second time logic had no place in his life. "Would it be more clear if I said I would love to be a part of your life?"

Her eyes widened and her head bobbed.

"Or that I need you in mine?" He shook his head. "Not to wait on me or fuss over my aches and pains, but to just be with me."

The slow dip of her chin was so long in coming that for a fraction in time he thought he'd just made the biggest mistake in his life.

In for a penny, in for a pound. "Or that I love everything about you?"

Delight replaced the wonder in her eyes, followed by a sweet smile. "Even if I keep trying to kill you?"

"You did not." He stopped and shook his head. "If you came at me with a butcher knife it wouldn't change a thing. I love you."

Lily flew in his direction, her arms settling around his neck. "And *that's* number three."

"Three?" He tipped his head back just enough to clearly read her face.

"All things come in three. My cookies are a hit. I'm going to get my dream bakery. And..." her smile widened, "the man I love loves me back."

"Loves you back?" How had he not read that? "I don't—"

Her finger landed on his lips. "Are you going to keep talking or are you going to kiss me?"

He didn't bother responding. Nudging her finger away, he eased forward and settled his mouth on hers. More addictive than her cookies, Lily was everything sweet and delicious life had to offer. As far as he was concerned, only one firefighter would be getting down on bending knee for her, and when he did, he wouldn't be joking. Far from it. He planned to keep catching her for the rest of his life.

CHAPTER TWENTY-ONE -

EPILOGUE

"It's almost time for the fireworks," Fiona Hart announced with the same enthusiasm she'd shown every New Year's Eve for as long as Violet could remember.

No matter how cold, and it got polar at the lake some years, the General always arranged for a nice show over the lake at exactly 12:01 am. The stroke of midnight was reserved for kissing his bride of decades.

"Those won't be the only fireworks," Cindy muttered, walking by Violet with a tray of roast pork. Another family tradition that the General and Grams had picked up during an overseas tour of duty was a midnight dinner on New Year's Eve. For a few years there were the twelve grapes in one minute at midnight. As kids, they all loved that one. Who could gobble them up the fastest had been a near vicious competition until Poppy choked on one and it was decided the family had plenty of good luck without the grapes.

Across the parlor, practically glued to the wall in the far corner, Lily was locking lips with her fireman. Despite the rocky start to the relationship, the pair made a good team. They brought balance into each other's lives. Especially Lily. Violet hadn't seen her trip over anything all week long.

"I detect a hint of green around those gills." This time Callie, following in Cindy's wake, muttered through one side of her mouth.

"Nope," Violet called after her cousin. "Just happy for them."

Callie stopped short and looked over at the pair who reluctantly pulled apart. "They really do look very happy. I would never have pictured my Easy Bake sister falling for a hot fireman, but it seems to be working."

Violet sighed. "Your sister and my sister seem to have found the holy grails when it comes to love."

"And what are you guys chatting about so seriously?" Rose held a large salad bowl.

"Love," the two cousins echoed.

Rose glanced at Lily and Cole chatting softly, holding hands while walking toward the porch for the upcoming show. "Ah. When I heard that the hunk had proposed on Christmas Eve, I thought this was all happening way too fast. But now I can see how perfect they are."

"I know what you mean." Cindy came back empty handed. "I half expected the two to come to dinner tonight and announce they'd eloped."

"I know!" Callie chimed in. "I thought the same thing!"

"Never happen." Violet shook her head. "Grams would be heartbroken to miss any of our weddings."

"And then there's Lucy," Rose added.

"Shh," a couple of the cousins whispered. "Don't let Lucy hear you mentioning the 'W' word or she'll have us surrounded by a brigade of fireman from the next county over."

"That might not be so bad." Rose glanced at Lily and Cole again.

Three sets of eyes glared at the redhead from New York. "Have you lost your mind?"

"What's wrong with a hunky fireman?" Rose asked.

"Nothing," Violet answered.

"But," Cindy shook her head, "this is Lucy we're talking about."

Rose seemed to ponder the statement for a minute and then, her forehead crinkling, nodded. "She does have a less than stellar reputation."

"Understatement," Violet said.

"Everyone to the porch!" the General barked. "Count down in 30."

Hurrying after their grandfather, all the cousins in attendance, a few close friends, and the new soon-to-be grandsons stepped outside, thanking the stars for the unseasonably warm night. Well, warm by Lawford standards. Bundled in sweaters and light jackets, the singles huddled near the heaters and the couples made their own heat.

"Ten, nine…" the General started. Violet moved closer to her sister Rose, watching her sister Heather with her fiancé, and her mom and dad, both couples holding hands and watching the sky.

"Eight, seven, six."

Violet and her sisters, her cousins too, had all been blessed with great role models for love. And she was truly happy that Heather and Lily both found men worthy of them.

"Three, two, one."

"Happy New Year" erupted all around her. Spinning to her sister, they hugged and then turned to the nearest cousin. Hugs and smiles abounded. Violet had barely managed to get in a hug with a handful of family when the explosion above sounded. Reds, blues, and whites filled the sky.

"You look lost, dear." Fiona Hart sidled up to her granddaughter.

"No. Just thinking. The bright lights look so beautiful against the velvet sky."

Grams nodded and looped an arm around Violet. "Your grandfather said it starts the New Year off with a bang. Literally. Ordinary troubles seem so small compared to the possibilities."

"I suppose it does."

"Of course it does. Life is all about balance. Nothing is ever all good or bad, all right or wrong. It's learning to find the point of equilibrium that brings joy into life."

"Equilibrium, huh?" Violet was pretty good at that. She could stand on one foot with her eyes closed for longer than anyone she knew, but somehow she didn't think that's what her grandmother was talking about.

Grams squeezed Violet tightly against her. "Come on, it's time for supper. If I do say so myself, the roast came out especially tender and the candied yams are making my mouth water."

"Always a good source of sugar overload." Violet leaned into her grandmother and smiled.

Grams held up one finger and kissed Violet on the cheek. "Remember what I said. Balance." Then she walked ahead.

Violet looked around the room of family she loved more than life itself. *Balance*. Definitely easier said than done.

From Lily's Recipe Box

SPITZBUBEN

What you'll need:

1 cup sugar
1 cup (2 sticks) + 2 Tablespoons salted butter
1 ½ cup ground walnuts
1 teaspoon vanilla
2 ¼ cups flour
Raspberry Jam
Instructions:

Cream the sugar & butter
Add nuts & vanilla.
Mix in flour.
Knead dough very well.
On lightly floured surface roll to 1/8" thick and cut with cookie cutter.
(we use small round and make bite-size)
Place on ungreased cookie sheet.
Bake at 350 degrees for 11 minutes or until lightly browned.
Cool.
Spread half cookies with raspberry jam and top with another cookie.
Dip into granulated sugar.

Makes about 5 dozen sandwiched cookies.

Enjoy!

Excerpt from VIOLET

"It will never work."
"Of course, it will."
"As much as I'd like to think you're right, I don't know."
"Well, I do. Sit back and see for yourself."

Scrambling to fit one more project into his already stretched to the limit schedule, the last thing Grant Whitaker needed was delays from a downpour to rival Hurricane Hilda.

The truck's speakers sounded an incoming call and without thinking he tapped the steering wheel to answer. "Whitaker."

"You staying dry?" his grandfather asked.

"Doing my best. How about you?"

"Your Grandmother didn't marry a fool. I know a good time to settle in with the sports channels." Low chatter from the television announcers hummed in the background. "Don't suppose you've found a good woman to keep you home?"

Grant opted to ignore the not so subtle jab at his bachelorhood. "On my way to a construction site. The retirement village. Phase one is ready for finishes. Phase two is framed and presales for the independent living have gone so well we're moving the groundbreaking up for the memory care unit."

"It was pretty smart of you to build the commercial side first. Most folks would have built the housing then added the shops."

"Where's the fun in doing things the way most people do it?" That was a phrase his grandfather had used so often in his life that it was a standing joke with the entire family.

His grandfather chuckled. "Won't get an argument out of me. Have you reached out to the General yet?"

"I've tried. For a retired man, he keeps himself hard to reach."

"That would be retired general. Sitting still isn't anything they do well. You didn't give up, did you?"

"No. I took your advice. Made reservations at the lake. I agree, deals like this are better fleshed out in person." Which was one of the reasons Grant was good at what he did. In a modern world of online meetings and texts, he understood the value of face to face contact. He'd been taught long ago that the best deals of his career would be made on the golf course. Same could be said over a cup of hot chocolate at a lakeside cabin. "It's why I'm driving in this mess. In order to carve out a couple of days I needed to bump a few things up on my schedule."

"Sounds good, but stay safe and when you get there, let me know if I should book your grandmother and me a cabin. I've heard a lot of nice things about Hart Land."

"Will do. Give Mums my love."

The call disconnected and Grant smiled to himself. His grandfather had taught him everything he knew about business long before Grant truly understood what was happening. If his grandfather's lead about the Hart Land was spot on, rearranging his plans to clear time to visit Retired Marine Corps General Harold Hart would be worth spending a few hours today impersonating a drowning rat. Every developer in the northeast knew the Hart family owned the single largest section of undeveloped waterfront land on popular Lake Lawford. Grant didn't need his Harvard degree to know this next deal could be the coup of the decade. The largest planned resort community in decades.

Through the sheets of rain, he slowed to spot the dirt road that led to the main construction site. It had taken two years to pull this not so little project off. At almost every turn the investors doubted his vision. Even his partner, Joe Fiorello, had bucked him on building commercial space first. In three states, Fiorello Construction might be the most recognizable name whenever a new building goes up, but it was Grant's eye for a deal and gift for making it happen that had put F&W Development Co. on the world map.

Despite sitting nearly a foot off the ground in his quad cab pickup, the pot holes from the large trucks hauling earth up and down this path had him rattling around like a kid at a birthday party bounce house. At least he knew a well-worn rut in the road meant that despite the weather's uncooperative nature, the work for the new phase was well underway.

"Hey, Mr. Whitaker. What brings you here on a day like today?" The security guard popped his head out of the small booth at the gate. The days when a construction site of this size could go unfenced were long gone. At this stage of the game a human face had to be added to the loss prevention plans.

"Just popping in for a quick check."

"Mr. Fiorello was here earlier this morning." A construction man to the bone, Joe could work through a typhoon if needed. Though Grant had no idea what would need him out here on a day like today.

"You stay dry, Jeff."

"Will do. You too." The man slid the glass window shut.

Thanks to the torrential downpour, the crew all toiled at the finishing work on the first condos. The man he wanted to check on would be in the office trailer. As soon as the rain stopped they'd be able to move out of the trailer and into the facilities office for the new maintenance building. The building at the rear of the compound would be used for storage as well. An extra layer of security. With little activity on this end of the site, and only the new site supervisor's truck in front, he parked his pickup near the entrance. A fresh gust of wind helped shove the narrow door wide open, blowing him and the rain inside.

"Grant?" Larry looked up, eyes brimming with surprise. "Didn't expect to see you here."

"Yeah, well." He shook off as much of the drenching as he could and walked over to the work table, leaving a trail of droplets in his wake. "I've got to head up north for a few days. This is the only time I could squeeze in coming by. How are you settling in?"

"Fine, thanks." The supervisor cast a quick glance out the window then back. No doubt thinking the same thing Grant did—what the hell did he think he could do on a day like today?

"The investors are all over me like white on rice. I've never seen such a jittery bunch. I need this next phase to go off without a hitch." Not even the dollar signs from hefty presales could squash the complaints of building too much too fast.

"Yeah," Larry nodded, "I heard."

Grant looked up from perusing the plans sprawled open on the table. Why had Larry heard? Grant was the only contact with the investors. Joe handled the construction and Grant handled the suits, having just enough interaction with the work sites to keep abreast.

"Something wrong?" Larry asked.

"No." Grant brushed off his concerns. Of course Larry knew about the investors. Even though he'd kept his reports to Joe at a minimum to avoid making his partner any more doubtful about the pace of this project then he already was, the PITA investors wasn't a secret. Especially with Larry; the guy had been supervisor on dozens of projects through the years and knew the business almost as well as he and Joe. Had saved their butts on this one, shifting projects at the last minute. "Should have had more coffee this morning."

The foreman moved from where he'd been standing next to Larry, filled a travel mug and handed it to Grant. "Fresh pot."

"Thanks." He practically inhaled the first long hot gulp. Definitely the elixir of the gods. How did anyone survive a work day without coffee? He loved watching a project grow from drawing to turn key. And F&W provided the epitome of turn key. The best quality guaranteed. And they charged for it too. "Are we still running ahead of schedule for the main building?"

Larry nodded. "Told Joe we should be delivering about two weeks early."

The size of his best supervisor's grin was no surprise. There were hefty bonuses for everyone if a project came in early. Grant believed in spreading the windfall around and every crew member knew it. He walked over to the tiny window in the trailer. From here all he could see was the excavation. "How far behind on phase three will this weather put us?"

"Hard to say. If the squall doesn't stall we'll be fine. If it sits over us for a few days, well, you know how that goes."

"Yeah." Phase one had gone surprisingly well despite the shift in supervisors. He'd never known a project not to run into a snafu of some sort and this particular project seemed to be running almost too good to be true. Maybe his luck was about to run out.

• • • •

"Namaste. And that's it for today." Violet clicked on the remote control, fading the music to silence.

"Will we still be here next week?" one of the two women in the class asked.

Pushing to her feet, the other woman shook her head. "I hope not. I never realized how spoiled I was having a yoga studio only a short walk from my apartment."

Boy, did Violet know that. In the time since her yoga studio had flooded, one by one, almost all her regular clients had found an excuse to skip class at her temporary location. She'd never realized how much of her customer base was due to convenience and not a reflection on her. "It doesn't sound like the old studio will be ready as quickly as I had hoped."

The first lady nodded, but her expression didn't look any more happy about the news than the other woman's.

"Perhaps I'll postpone classes until further notice." She wished the two ladies didn't look so pleased with that announcement. "You can continue to stretch on your own and as soon as we're up and running again I'll send out notifications."

Grinning from ear to ear, the ladies bobbed their heads and gathered their belongings. Violet hoped silently that by the time the studio was open again she still had a client base and wouldn't have to start her business from scratch.

"See you soon," the shorter blonde waved.

"We hope," the other woman added.

A towel in one hand, Violet forced a smile and waved with her free hand. Her mat rolled up and her belongings somewhat neatly tucked in her bag, she looked around the place and wondered now what? Mrs. Renfru was what. The building owner had not uttered a word in over a week. Giving the woman her space to deal with a difficult situation was one thing, but it was definitely time for Violet to speak up. After all, if she needed to find a new permanent location, the sooner the better.

Scrolling through her contacts in search of Renfru, the phone buzzed and the screen lit up with the landlady's name. Maybe the universe was finally on her side. "Hello, Mrs. Renfru."

"Hello, Violet. You always sound so nice and relaxed."

"Thank you." She'd worked hard most of her life to not allow the chaos of a busy city like Boston to steal her peace. Despite the upbeat words, something in her landlady's tone left Violet unsure that right now she'd be able to win that particular battle. "What news do you have?"

"I'm afraid it's not good."

Oh, how Violet hated it when her gut instinct and her peace of mind collided.

"It seems that after the water cleanup, the company found traces of mold."

Alarm bells rang loud and clear in Violet's ear.

"Enough that they had to call in someone to test. That's what's been taking so long."

Nothing about this woman's tone of voice was reassuring.

"All the ground floor space affected by the flood needs to have mold remediation. Thankfully that much is actually covered by my insurance policy. At least most of it."

Okay, Violet felt some of the tension in her shoulders ease. That wasn't as bad as she had braced herself for.

"But not the electrical."

"Electrical?"

"The water damaged some of the wiring. The insurance will cover the damaged wiring but according to the electrician's estimate, once he touches any of the wiring, he's required to bring the entire building up to code."

And the other shoe came crashing down with the full weight of Jack's giant.

"I simply can't afford to do that. Not to mention once we start opening up walls, who knows what else they'll find. Without the updates the city won't issue a certificate of occupancy for the retail spaces."

"No." Hands full, Violet sank to the floor in a butterfly pose. "I can see where that's a problem."

"I need the rental income. I can't—won't—raise the tenants' rents enough to offset the losses."

Thank heaven for that. Violet's rent hadn't gone up in all the years she'd lived in Mrs. Renfru's building. Though she suspected it was because of what she paid for the studio.

"I'm considering selling the building."

And that would be a locked and loaded guarantee of her rents for both the apartment and the studio skyrocketing.

"My only other option is a loan from the bank, but frankly I don't know if that will work for me. I'm not as young as I used to be."

"You're as young as you feel, Mrs. Renfru." And the woman did seriously look a decade younger than her years.

"Yes, well today I'm feeling ancient. I'm sorry to keep you in limbo, but as soon as I have this together, I'll let you know."

"Thank you, Mrs. Renfru. And make sure to take care of yourself." The situation might be messy, but that didn't change the fact that her landlady was a likeable old woman. "Worrying won't change anything."

"No dear, no it won't."

Lifting to her feet, Violet disconnected the call and slid the phone into her bag. She needed to follow her own advice. Worrying wasn't going to do anyone a bit of good. Planning, on the other hand, that was something her mother and father had drummed into her from the cradle. One of the many reasons she was able to have her own yoga studio at her age. Unfortunately, rewiring a building was not anywhere in those plans. Maybe she should ask her dad to help Mrs. Renfru. After all, what good was having banking connections if you didn't pull a few strings now and then? And though she'd promised herself she wasn't going to worry, she liked the idea of Mrs. Renfru fixing up the place a whole lot better than she liked the idea of a new landlord.

Violet pulled the glass door shut behind her and turned the lock. Her phone buzzed. Missed call from her grandmother. She let out a heavy sigh. What she needed now was a little of Lily's chocolate chip banana bread, Lucy's garlic shrimp, and her grandmother's smile. Not necessarily in that order. A bonfire on the beach with her cousins wouldn't hurt either, even if it was freezing outside.

Checking the time on her cell, Violet did some fast math. If she hurried home, by the time she showered and threw a few things into a bag, the height of rush hour would be over and she could make it to the lake by the first deal of the cards. The thought brought a smile to her face. She'd spent more weekends on the lake the past few months than she had in all of the last couple of years. Whatever changes this temporary setback brought, the bright side would be a plan that included more time at the lake. Yep, she could feel her Zen returning. Everything would work itself out. She was sure. She couldn't afford not to be.

Available at your favorite bookseller.

MEET CHRIS

USA TODAY Bestselling Author of more than a dozen contemporary novels, including the award-winning *Champagne Sisterhood*, Chris Keniston lives in suburban Dallas with her husband, two human children, and two canine children. Though she loves her puppies equally, she admits being especially attached to her German Shepherd rescue. After all, even dogs deserve a happily ever after.

More on Chris and her books can be found at
www.chriskeniston.com

Follow Chris on Facebook at ChrisKenistonAuthor
or on Twitter @ckenistonauthor

Questions? Comments?
I would love to hear from you.
You can reach me at chris@chriskeniston.com